Jess felt as ~~if the ground was~~ tipping beneath her feet.

If she could just reach out a hand she could feel him. See if he really was real. But she couldn't move. Life seemed to be going on around her as she watched, too overcome to react.

Lucas turned towards her at the sound of his name.

'JJ?'

She hadn't been called JJ in years. She couldn't believe he was standing in front of her. Lucas—undeniably Lucas. He still had the same brilliant forget-me-not-blue eyes and the same infectious dimpled smile as he stepped forward and wrapped her in a hug. She fitted perfectly into his embrace and it felt as if it was only yesterday that she'd last been in his arms. Memories flooded back to her and her stomach did a peculiar little flip as her body responded in a way it hadn't for years. She tensed, her reaction taking her by surprise.

He must have felt her stiffen because he let her go and stepped away.

Her heart raced as she looked him over. He looked just ~~as she remembered~~. Maybe ev~~en~~

Dear Reader,

I can't believe that after twenty-one books this is my first story with a Christmas theme—and not just *any* Christmas but a white one!

White Christmases are a foreign concept to most Australians—for us it is the subject matter of fairy tales and dreams. Although I'm sure most of us would say it is something we'd love to experience. Many years ago I was lucky enough to spend a winter in Canada. While minus seventeen degrees Celsius wasn't quite what I had imagined, it was a novelty to listen to Christmas carols about reindeers, snow and sleigh bells while I was surrounded by ice and snow instead of at a hot, sandy beach.

I love Christmas, and I love summer, but there's no denying that a wintry Christmas, complete with sleigh rides, open fires and fir trees decorated with lights and a dusting of snow, is very romantic—and I did enjoy setting the scene for Jess and Lucas's own fairy-tale Christmas.

I hope you enjoy their story and, wherever you may be in the world, I wish you a very Merry Christmas!

Emily

HIS LITTLE CHRISTMAS MIRACLE

BY
EMILY FORBES

Published in Great Britain 2015
by Mills & Boon, an imprint of Harlequin (UK) Limited,
Eton House, 18-24 Paradise Road, Richmond, Surrey, TW9 1SR

© 2015 Emily Forbes

ISBN: 978-0-263-24737-4

Harlequin (UK) Limited's policy is to use papers that are natural, renewable and recyclable products and made from wood grown in sustainable forests. The logging and manufacturing processes conform to the legal environmental regulations of the country of origin.

Printed and bound in Spain
by CPI, Barcelona

Emily Forbes is an award-winning author of Harlequin Mills & Boon® Medical Romance™. She has written over 20 books and has twice been a finalist in the Australian Romantic Book of the Year Award, which she won in 2013 for her novel *Sydney Harbour Hospital: Bella's Wishlist*. You can get in touch with Emily at emilyforbes@internode.on.net, or visit her website at emily-forbesauthor.com

**Visit the author profile page at
millsandboon.co.uk for more titles**

Emily Forbes won the
2013 Australian Romantic Book of the Year Award
for her title *Sydney Harbour Hospital: Bella's Wishlist*

PROLOGUE

'AND SO IT BEGINS,' Kristie said as she stuck her head into her cousin's bedroom.

'So what begins?' Jess asked as she tied off her plaits and pulled a red knitted hat over her white-blonde hair. She picked up her sunglasses and ski gloves and followed her cousin out of their family's five-star apartment.

'Operation Find Jess a Boyfriend,' Kristie replied.

'What! Why?'

'Because you're almost eighteen and you have no idea what you've been missing. It's time to find you a gorgeous boy. One you won't be able to resist, someone who can kiss their way into that ivory tower of yours and sweep you off your feet. We've talked about this.'

They had but Kristie was always talking about boys in one way or another and Jess mostly ignored her. Kristie was boy crazy—she fell in love every couple of weeks—but Jess was different. Most boys Jess met seemed immature and silly. She didn't see what all the fuss was about. Seventeen- and eighteen-year-old boys were just that. Boys. And Jess wanted Prince Charming. And Prince Charming would arrive in his own time. She didn't think Kristie was going to be able to conjure him up.

'I think you're forgetting something,' Jess said as they dropped their skis onto the snow and clicked their boots into the bindings, ready to tackle their first day on the slopes of the Moose River Alpine Resort.

'What's that?'

'I'd never be allowed to find my own boyfriend. Everyone I've ever dated has been a friend of the family.'

'*You're* not going to find him, I'm going to find him for you,' Kristie explained. 'And let's be honest, you'll never get laid if you only date guys your dad picks out. For one they'd be too terrified of what he'd do to them if he found out and, two, I'm sure your dad deliberately picks guys who are potentially gay.'

'That's not true,' Jess retorted even as she wondered whether maybe it was.

But surely not? Some of those boys had kissed her and while the experiences certainly hadn't been anything to rave about she'd always thought that was her fault. The boys had been cute enough, polite and polished in a typical trust-fund, private-school, country-club way, but not one of them had ever set her heart racing or made her feel breathless or excited or any of the things she'd expected to feel or wanted to feel, and she'd decided she was prepared to wait for the right one.

'Maybe I don't want a boyfriend,' she added.

'Maybe not, but you definitely need to get laid.'

'Kristie!' Jess was horrified.

'You don't know what you're missing. That's going to be my eighteenth birthday present to you. I'm going to find you a gorgeous boy and you're going to get laid.'

Kristie laughed but Jess suspected she wasn't joking. Kristie didn't see anything wrong with advertising the fact that she wanted to hook up with a boy but Jess could think of nothing more embarrassing. Despite the fact that they spent so much time together their personalities were poles apart. Less than three months separated them in age but Kristie was far savvier than Jess, not to mention more forthright and confident.

'This is your chance,' Kristie continued. 'We have one week before your parents arrive. One week with just my parents, who are nowhere near as strict. That's seven days to check out all the hot guys who'll just be hanging around the resort. You'll never get a better opportunity to hook up with someone.'

'Maybe I don't want to hook up with anyone. Promise me you won't set me up,' Jess begged. Kristie's seven-day deadline coincided with Jess's eighteenth birthday. Her parents were coming up to the resort to celebrate it with her and once they arrived Jess knew she wouldn't have a chance to be alone with a boy. Surely not even Kristie could make this happen in such a short time even if Jess *was* a willing participant. And while she wasn't averse to the *idea* of the experience, she wanted it her way. She wanted the romance. She wanted to fall in love. She wanted to be seduced and made love to. *Getting laid* did not have the same ring. Getting laid was not the experience she was after.

But then she relaxed. She might get a chance to kiss a boy but even though Kristie's parents were far more lenient than her own she still doubted that she would get an opportunity to lose her virginity.

'We won't be allowed out at night,' she said when Kristie didn't answer.

Kristie laughed again. 'Do you think you're only allowed to have sex after midnight?' she called back over her shoulder as she skied over to join the lift line for the village quad chair. 'No one is keeping tabs on us during the day. We could sneak off whenever we wanted.'

Sex during the day! Jess hadn't considered that possibility. But it still wasn't going to happen. As much as Kristie wanted her project to get off the ground, Jess couldn't imagine getting naked in the middle of the day. In her fantasy she imagined soft lighting, perfumed candles, the right music and a comfortable bed. Preferably her own bed. With clean sheets and a man who adored her. A quick fumble in the middle of the day with some random guy from the resort, no matter how cute, just wasn't the same thing.

'Today is the beginning of the rest of your life. It's time you had some fun,' Kristie told her as she joined the line. 'This place will be crawling with good-looking boys. We'll be able to take our pick.'

Getting a boy's attention was never a problem. Jess knew she was pretty enough. She was petite, only one hundred and sixty centimetres tall, and cheerleader pretty with a heart-shaped face, a chin she thought was maybe a bit too pointy, platinum-blonde hair, green eyes and porcelain skin. Finding a boy who ticked all her boxes was the tricky part. And if one did measure up then getting a chance to be alone was another challenge entirely.

Kristie's joke about Jess's ivory tower wasn't completely inaccurate. Jess did have dreams of being swept off her feet, falling madly in love and being rescued from her privileged but restricted life. It seemed to be her best chance of escaping the rules and boundaries her parents imposed on her. She couldn't imagine gaining her freedom any other way. She wasn't rebellious enough to go against their wishes without very good reason.

But she couldn't imagine falling in love at the age of seventeen and she wasn't about to leap into bed with the first cute guy who presented her with the opportunity. That didn't fit with her romantic notions at all. But although Jess could protest vigorously, it didn't mean Kristie would give up. And she proved it with her next comment.

'What about him?' she asked as they waited for the quad chair.

Jess looked at the other skiers around them. It was just after nine in the morning. The girls had risen early, keen to enjoy their first morning on the slopes, but everyone else in the line was ten years younger or twenty years older than them. They were surrounded by families with young children. All the other teenagers were still in bed, and Jess couldn't work out who Kristie was talking about.

Her cousin nudged her in the side. 'There.' She used her ski pole to point to the front of the line and Jess realised she meant the towies.

Two young men, who she guessed to be a year or two older than she was, worked the lift together. They both wore the uniform of the mountain resort, bright blue ski jackets with a band of fluorescent yellow around the upper arm and matching blue pants with another yellow band around the bottom of the legs. A row of white, snow-covered mountain peaks was stitched across the left chest of the jacket with 'Moose River Alpine Resort' emblazoned beneath. Their heads were uncovered and Jess could see one tall, fair-headed boy and another slightly shorter one with dark hair.

They had music pumping out of the stereo system at the base of the lift. It blasted the mountain, drowning out all other noise, including the engine of the chairlift. Jess watched as the boys danced to the beat as they lifted the little kids onto the chair and chatted and flirted with the mothers.

The fair one drew her attention. He moved easily, in time with the music, relaxed, unselfconscious and comfortable in his skin. Jess couldn't ever imagine dancing in front of strangers in broad daylight. She wasn't comfortable in a crowd. But there was something erotic about watching someone dance from a distance. She wouldn't normally stare but she was emboldened by her anonymity. He didn't know her and from behind the security of her dark sunglasses she could watch unobserved. Like a voyeur.

Kristie shuffled forward in the line and Jess followed but she couldn't tear her eyes away from the dancing towie. Watching the way his hips moved, she felt a stirring in her belly that she recognised as attraction, lust, desire. Watching him move, she could imagine how it would feel to dance with him, how it would feel to be held against him as his hips moved in time with hers. She found her hips swaying to the beat of the music, swaying in response to this stranger.

The song changed, snapping her out of her reverie, and she watched as he mimicked some rap moves that had the kids in front of her in stitches. The dark-haired one was chatting to a mother while the fair one lifted the woman's child onto the seat before giving him a high five. He lifted his head as he laughed at something the child had said and suddenly he was looking straight at Jess.

Jess's pulse throbbed and her stomach ached with a primal, lustful reaction as his eyes connected with hers. They were the most brilliant blue. A current tore through her body, sending a shock deep inside her all the way to her bones. She was aware of Kristie moving into position for the lift but she was riveted to the spot, her skis frozen to the snow. She was transfixed by eyes the colour of forget-me-nots.

'Careful. Keep moving unless you want to get collected by the chair.' It took Jess a second or two to realise he was talking to her. He had an Australian accent and in her bewildered and confused state it took her a moment to decipher it and make sense of his words. While she was translating his speech in her head he reached out and put one hand on her backside and pushed her forward until she was standing on the mat, ready to be swept up by the chairlift. Jess could swear she could feel the heat of his hand through the padding of her ski suit. She was still standing in place, staring at him, as the chair swung behind her and scooped her up, knocking into the back of her knees and forcing her to sit down with a thump.

'Have a good one.' He winked at her as she plopped into the seat and Jess felt herself blush but she kept eye contact. She couldn't seem to look away. *Let me off*, she wanted to shout but when she opened her mouth nothing came out. Her eyesight worked but she appeared to have lost control of all her other senses. Including movement. She was enchanted, spellbound by a boy with eyes of blue.

'They were cute,' Kristie said as the lift carried them up the mountain and Jess forced herself to turn her head and look away. Maybe that would break the spell.

'I guess,' she said. She felt like she had a mouthful of marbles as she tried to feign indifference. Kristie would have a field day if she knew what Jess had really been thinking.

'What do you think?' Kristie asked. 'Worth a second look?'

The girls had the quad chair to themselves but that didn't mean Jess wanted to have this discussion. She knew if she agreed it would only serve to encourage Kristie's foolish plan.

'You're not serious!' she cried. 'I don't think they're my type.' She suspected she'd have nothing in common with them. She knew she wouldn't be cool enough.

'Why not?'

'You know the reputation those guys have.' The towies—usually an assortment of college students taking a gap year, locals and backpackers—had a reputation as ski-hard-and-party-harder people.

But Kristie was not about to be deterred. 'So...' she shrugged '...that all adds to the excitement and the challenge.'

'I'm not going to hook up with a total stranger,' Jess said. Obviously the lessons of her upbringing were more deeply ingrained in her than she'd realised. Her movements were carefully orchestrated, her whereabouts were always mapped out, and she'd never really had the opportunity to mingle with strangers. Prince Charming was going to have his work cut out for him.

'I know your parents want to know where you are every minute of the day but they're not here,' Kristie replied, 'and despite what they tell you, not every spontaneous situation is dangerous and not every stranger is a psychopath. I'm not saying you have to marry the guy, just have some fun.'

'He looked too old for me,' Jess protested.

'You're always complaining about how immature boys our age are. Maybe someone a bit older would suit you better. Shall we head back down? Take another look?'

The quad chair took them to the basin where all the other lifts operated from. No one skied straight back down to the bottom of this lift unless they'd forgotten something and needed to return to the village. Jess didn't want to be that overtly interested. She needed time to think. 'No. I want to ski,' she said as they were deposited in the basin.

The slopes were quiet at this hour of the day and it wasn't long before Kristie decided she was overheating from all the exercise and needed to discard some layers. Jess suspected it was all an act designed to invent a reason to return to their apartment and hence to the quad chair, but she was prepared to give in. She knew she didn't have much choice. She could have elected to stay up on the mountain but they had a rule that no one skied alone and she had to admit she was just a tiny bit curious to have another look at the boy with the forget-me-not-blue eyes. After all, there was no harm in looking.

But by the time they had changed their outfits and returned to the quad chair there were two different towies on duty. Disappointment surged through Jess. It was silly to feel that way about a random stranger but there had been something hypnotic about him. Something captivating.

They rode the lift back to the basin where they waited in line for another quad chair to take them to the top of the ski run. As they neared the front the two original towies appeared, each with a snowboard strapped to one foot as they slipped into the singles row and skated to the front of the line.

'G'day. Mind if we join you?'

Jess and Kristie had no time to reply before the boys had slotted in beside them and Jess found herself sandwiched between her cousin and the boy with the tousled, blond hair and amazing blue eyes. He shifted slightly on the seat, turning a little to face her, and the movement pushed his thigh firmly against hers.

'Have you had a good morning?' he asked her. 'You were up at sparrow's.'

'Pardon?' Jess frowned. His voice was deep and his accent was super-sexy but the combination of his stunning eyes and his Aussie drawl made it difficult to decipher his words. Or maybe it was just the fact that she was sitting thigh to thigh with a cute boy who was messing with her head. Either way, she couldn't think straight and she could make no sense of what he was saying.

'Sparrow's fart,' he said with a grin before he elaborated. 'It means you were up really early.'

His blue eyes sparkled as he smiled at her but this time it was the twin dimples in his cheeks that set Jess's heart racing. His smile was infectious and she couldn't help but return it as she said, 'You remember us?' She was surprised and flattered. The boys would have seen hundreds of people already today.

'Of course. Don't tell me you don't remember me?' He put both hands over his heart and looked so dramatically wounded that Jess laughed. She'd have to watch out—he was cute and charming with more than a hint of mischief about him.

And, of course, she remembered him. She doubted she'd ever forget him, but she knew his type and she wasn't about to stroke his ego by telling him that his eyes were the perfect colour—unforgettable, just like him. She knew all the towies were cut from the same cloth, young men who would spend the winter working in the resort and then spend their time off skiing and drinking and chasing girls. They would flirt with dozens of girls in one day, trying their luck, until eventually their persistence would pay off and they'd have a date for the night and, no matter how cute he was, she didn't want to be just another girl in the long line that would fall at his feet.

'Well, just so you don't forget us again, I'm Lucas and that's Sam,' he said, nodding towards his mate, who was sitting on the other side of Kristie.

'I didn't say I'd forgotten you,' Jess admitted. 'I remember your accent.' But she wasn't prepared to admit she remembered his dancing or had been unable to forget his cornflower-blue eyes. 'You're Australian?'

'Yes, and, before you ask, I don't have a pet kangaroo.'

'I wasn't going to ask that.'

'Really?'

'I might not have been to Australia but I know a bit about it. I'm not completely ignorant.'

'Sorry, I didn't mean to imply that,' Lucas backtracked.

'It's okay.' She'd stopped getting offended every time people treated her like a cheerleader but while she was one she was also a science major. 'I know most of you don't have pet kangaroos and I know you eat that horrible black spread on your toast and live alongside loads of poisonous snakes, spiders and man-eating sharks. Actually…' she smiled '…I'm not surprised you left.'

Lucas laughed. 'I'm not here permanently. I'm only here for the winter. It's summer back home. I'll stay until the end of February when uni starts again.'

'So where is the best place to party in the village?' Kristie interrupted. 'What's popular this season?'

Kristie knew the village as well as anyone—she didn't need advice—but Jess knew it was just her cousin's way of flirting. To Kristie that came as naturally as breathing.

'How old are you?' Sam replied.

'Nineteen,' she fibbed. She was only three months older than Jess and had only recently turned eighteen but nineteen was the legal drinking age.

'The T-Bar is always good,' Sam told them, mentioning one of the après-ski bars that had been around for ever but was always popular.

'But tonight we're having a few mates around,' Lucas added. 'We're sharing digs with a couple of Kiwis and Friday nights are party nights. You're welcome to join us.'

'Thanks, that sounds like fun,' Kristie replied, making it sound as though they'd be there when Jess knew they wouldn't. Which was a pity. It did sound like it might be fun but there was no way they'd be allowed out with strangers, with boys who hadn't been vetted and approved. Although Kristie's parents weren't as strict as hers, Jess's aunt and uncle knew the rules Jess had to live by and she didn't think they'd bend them that far.

'We're in the Moose River staff apartments. You know the ones? On Slalom Street. Apartment fifteen.'

'We know where they are.'

They were almost at the top of the ski run now and Jess felt a surge of disappointment that the ride was coming to an end. The boys were going snowboarding and Jess assumed they'd be heading to the half-pipe or the more rugged terrain on the other side of the resort.

They wouldn't be skiing the same part of the mountain as she and Kristie.

She pretended to look out at the ski runs when she was actually looking at Lucas from behind the safety of her sunglasses. She wanted to commit his face to memory. He was cute and friendly but she doubted she'd ever see him again. He wasn't her Prince Charming.

CHAPTER ONE

JESS ZIPPED UP her ski jacket as she stood in the twilight. She was back.

Back in the place where her life had changed for ever. Back in Moose River.

She remembered standing not far from this exact spot while Kristie had told her that day marked the beginning of the rest of her life, but she hadn't expected her cousin's words to be quite so prophetic. That had been the day she'd met Lucas and her life had very definitely changed. All because of a boy.

Jess shoved her hands into her pockets and stood still as she took in her surroundings. The mountain village was still very familiar but it was like an echo of a memory from a lifetime ago. A very different lifetime from the one she was living now. She took a deep breath as she tried to quell her nerves.

When she had seen the advertisement for the position of clinic nurse at the Moose River Medical Centre it had seemed like a sign and she'd wondered why she hadn't thought of it sooner. It had seemed like the perfect opportunity to start living the life she wanted but that didn't stop the butterflies in her stomach.

It'll be fine, she told herself as she tried to get the butterflies to settle, *once we adjust*.

In the dark of the evening the mountain resort looked exactly like it always had. Like a fairy-tale village. The streets had been cleared of the early season snow and it lay piled in small drifts by the footpaths. Light dotted the hillside, glowing yellow as it spilled from the windows of the hotels and lodges. She could smell wood smoke and pine needles. The fragrance of winter. Of Christmas. Of Lucas.

She'd have to get over that. She couldn't afford to remember him every few minutes now that she was back here. That wasn't what this move was about.

In a childhood marked by tragedy and, at times, fear and loneliness, Moose River had been one of the two places where she'd been truly happy, the only place in the end, and the only place where she'd been free. She had returned now, hoping to rediscover that feeling again. And while she couldn't deny that Moose River was also full of bittersweet memories, she hoped it could still weave its magic for her.

She could hear the bus wheezing and shuddering behind her, complaining as the warmth from its air-conditioning escaped into the cold mountain air. It was chilly but at least it wasn't raining. She was so sick of rain. While Vancouver winters were generally milder than in other Canadian cities there was a trade-off and that was rain. While she was glad she didn't have to shovel snow out of her driveway every morning, she was tired of the wet.

Jess could hear laughter and music. The sound floated across to the car park from the buildings around her, filling the still night air. She could hear the drone of the snow-making machines on the mountain and she could see the lights of the graders as they went about their night-time business, grooming the trails. She glanced around her, looking to see what had changed and what had stayed the same in the seven years since she had last been here. The iconic five-star Moose River Hotel still had pride of place on the hill overlooking the village but there were several new buildings as well, including a stunning new hotel that stood at the opposite end of Main Street from the bus depot.

The new hotel was perched on the eastern edge of the plaza where Main Street came to an end at the ice-skating rink. There had been a building there before, smaller and older. Jess couldn't recall exactly what it had been but this modern replacement looked perfect. The hotel was too far away for her to be able to read the sign, although she could see the tiny figures of skaters gliding around the rink, twirling under the lights as snow began to fall.

She lifted her face to the sky. Snowflakes fell on her cheeks and eyelashes, melting as soon as they touched the warmth of her skin. She stuck out her tongue, just like she'd done as a child, and caught the flakes, feeling them immediately turn to water.

But she wasn't a child any more. She was twenty-four years old, almost twenty-five. Old enough to have learned that life was not a fairy tale. She didn't want a fairy-tale ending; she didn't believe in those any more but surely it wasn't too late to find happiness? She refused to believe that wasn't possible.

Seven years ago she'd had the world at her feet. She'd been young and full of expectation, anticipation and excitement. Anything had seemed possible in that winter.

In the winter that she'd met Lucas. In the winter that she'd fallen in love.

Sometimes it seemed like yesterday. At other times a lifetime ago. On occasions it even seemed like it was someone else's story but she knew it was hers. She was reminded of that every day. But as hard as it had been she wasn't sure that she would do anything differently if she had her time again.

She could still remember the first moment she had laid eyes on him. It was less than two hundred metres from where she now stood. She'd been seventeen years old, young and pretty, shy but with the self-assurance that a privileged lifestyle gave to teenagers. In her mind her future had already been mapped out—surely it would be one of happiness, wealth, prosperity and pleasure. That was what she and her friends, all of whom came from wealthy families, had been used to and they'd had no reason to think things would change. She'd been so naive.

At seventeen she'd had no clue about real life. She'd been happy with her dreams. Her biggest problem had been having parents who'd loved her and wanted to protect her from the world, and her biggest dream had been to experience the world she hadn't been allowed to taste.

To her, Lucas had represented freedom. He'd been her chance to experience the world but the freedom she'd tasted had been short-lived. And the real world was a lot tougher than she'd anticipated. Reality had slapped her in the face big time and once she'd been out in that world she'd found there had been no turning back.

Reality was a bitch and it had certainly killed her

naivety. She'd grown up awfully quickly and her clueless teenage years were a long way behind her now.

She was still standing in the car park, mentally reminiscing about that winter, when an SUV pulled up in front of her at a right angle to the bus. The driver put down his window. 'Jess? Jess Johnson?' he said.

Jess shook her head, clearing the cobwebs from her mind. 'Sorry,' the driver said, misinterpreting the shake of her head. 'I'm looking for a Jess Johnson.'

'That's me.'

The driver climbed out of the car. 'I'm Cameron Baker,' he introduced himself as he shook Jess's hand. Cameron and his wife, Ellen, owned the Moose River Medical Centre. He was Jess's new boss. 'Let's get your gear loaded up. Is this everything?'

Jess looked down at her feet. The bus driver had unloaded her belongings. Three suitcases and half a dozen boxes were piled beside her. All the necessities for two lives.

'That's it,' she replied. 'I'll just get Lily.'

She climbed back into the bus to rouse her sleeping daughter.

She scooped Lily up and carried her from the bus. She was keen to introduce her to Moose River but that would have to wait until tomorrow.

This was Lily's first visit to the mountain resort. Jess had avoided bringing Lily here before now. She'd made countless excuses, telling herself Lily was too young to appreciate it, but she knew that was a lie. Jess had been skiing since she was four and Lily was now six and there were plenty of other activities here to keep young children entertained for days. Lack of money had been another excuse and even though Jess hadn't been able to afford to bring her that was still only part of the truth. The reality was that Jess hadn't wanted to return. She hadn't wanted to face the past. She'd thought the memories might be too painful. But it was time to give Lily a sense of where she had come from. It was time to come back.

Cameron loaded their bags and Jess climbed into the back of the vehicle, cradling a sleepy Lily in her arms as he drove them the short distance to their accommodation. The job came with a furnished apartment, which had been one of a number of things that had attracted Jess to the position, but she hadn't thought to enquire about any specifics, she'd just been relieved to know it had been organised for her and she was stunned when Cameron pulled to a stop in front of the Moose River staff apartments.

She picked Lily up again—fortunately Lily was small for her age and Jess could still manage to carry her— and followed Cameron inside the building, counting off the apartment numbers as they walked down the corridor. Thirteen, fourteen, fifteen. Cameron's steps started to slow and Jess held her breath. It couldn't be. Not the same apartment.

'This is you. Number sixteen.'

She let out her breath as Cameron parked the luggage trolley, loaded with boxes and bags, and unlocked the door. There'd been a brief moment when she'd thought she might be staying in apartment fifteen but she might just be able to handle being one apartment away from her past.

She carried Lily inside and put her on the bed.

'I'm sorry, they were supposed to split the bed and

make up two singles,' Cameron apologised when he saw the bedding configuration.

'It doesn't matter,' Jess replied. 'I'll fix it tomorrow.' She couldn't be bothered now. She had enough to think about without fussing about the bed. She and Lily could manage for the night.

'Ellen has left some basic supplies for you in the fridge. She promised me it would be enough to get you through breakfast in the morning,' Cameron said, as he brought in the rest of Jess's luggage.

'That's great, thank you.'

'I'll let you get settled, then, and we'll see you at the clinic at eleven tomorrow to introduce you to everyone and give you an orientation.'

Jess nodded but she was having trouble focusing. She was restless. There were so many memories. Too many. More than she'd expected. Thank goodness Lily was dozing as that gave her a chance to shuffle through the thoughts that were crowding her brain. She paced around the apartment once Cameron had gone but it was tiny and in no more than a few steps she'd covered the kitchen and the dining area and the lounge. All that was left was the bedroom and a combined bathroom-laundry. There wasn't much to see and even less to do as she didn't want to disturb Lily by beginning to unpack.

She crossed the living room, opened the balcony doors and stepped outside. Night had fallen but a full moon hung low in the sky and moonlight reflected off the snow and lit up the village as if it was broad daylight. To her left was the balcony of unit fifteen, the two-bedroom apartment that Lucas had stayed in seven years ago. The apartment where she and Kristie had gone on the night of the party was only metres away.

She could see the exact spot where she'd been standing when Lucas had first kissed her.

He had been her first love. He had been her Prince Charming. She'd fallen hard and fast but when he'd kissed her that first time and she'd given him her heart she hadn't known there would be no turning back.

Now, at twenty-four, she didn't believe in Prince Charming any more.

CHAPTER TWO

'MUMMY?'

The sound of Lily's voice startled her. Jess was still on the balcony, standing with her fingers pressed against her lips as she recalled the first kiss she and Lucas had shared. She shivered as she realised she was freezing. She had no idea how long she'd been standing out there in the cold.

She didn't have time for reminiscing. She had responsibilities.

Lily had wandered out of the bedroom and Jess could see her standing in the living room, looking around at the unfamiliar surroundings. She was sucking on her thumb and had her favourite toy, a soft, grey koala, tucked under one arm. With white-blonde hair and a heart-shaped face she was the spitting image of Jess, just as Jess was the image of her own mother.

'I'm hungry,' Lily said, as Jess came in from the balcony and closed the doors and curtains behind her.

'You are?' She was surprised. Lily wasn't often hungry. She was a fussy eater and didn't have a good appetite and Jess often struggled to find food that appealed to her daughter, although fortunately she would eat her vegetables.

'Let's see what we've got.' Jess opened the fridge, hoping Cameron had been right when he'd said that his wife had left some basics for them. She could see bread, milk, eggs, cheese and jam.

'How about toasted cheese sandwiches for dinner?' she said. 'Or eggs and soldier toast?'

'Eggs and soldier toast.'

Jess put the eggs on to boil and then found Lily's pyjamas. By the time she was changed the eggs were done. Lily managed to finish the eggs and one soldier. Jess slathered the remaining soldier toasts with jam and polished them off herself.

Lily was fast asleep within minutes of climbing back into bed, but even though Jess was exhausted she found she couldn't get comfortable. Lily, who was a restless sleeper at the best of times, was tossing and turning in the bed beside her and disturbing her even further. She would have to split the bed apart tomorrow; she couldn't stand another night like this.

She got up and put the kettle on, hoping for the hundredth time that she'd made the right decision in moving to Moose River.

It seemed surreal to think that returning to the place where things had started to go wrong had been the best solution, but she'd felt she hadn't had much choice. She'd needed a job with regular hours and this one had the added bonus of accommodation, which meant she could be home with Lily before and after school and she wouldn't need to leave Lily with a childminder or take extra shifts to cover the rent or babysitting expenses. She also hoped that living in Moose River would give Lily the opportunity to have the childhood she herself had missed out on. A childhood free from worry, a childhood of fun and experiences.

She carried her decaf coffee over to the balcony doors. She drew back the curtains and rested her head on the glass as she gazed out at the moonlit night and let the memories flood back. Of course they were all about Lucas. She couldn't seem to keep thoughts of him out of her head. She hadn't expected Moose River to stir her memory quite so much.

What would he be looking at right now? Where would he be?

Probably living at Bondi Beach, running a chain of organic cafés with his gorgeous bikini-model wife, she thought. They would have three blue-eyed children and together his family would look like an advertisement for the wonders of fresh air and exercise and healthy living.

But maybe life hadn't been so kind to him. Why should it have been? Why should he be glowing with health and happiness?

Perhaps he was working in a hotel restaurant in the Swiss Alps and had grown fat from over-indulging in cheese and chocolate. He could be overweight with a receding hairline. Would that make her feel better?

What was it she wanted to feel better about? she wondered. It didn't matter where Lucas was or what he was doing. That was history. She'd woken up to herself in the intervening years. Woken up to real life. And he wasn't part of that life. He was fantasy, not reality. Not her reality anyway.

Jess shook herself. She needed to get a grip. Her situation was entirely of her own choosing and she wouldn't change it for anything, not if it meant losing Lily.

She sighed as she finished her coffee. Her father had

been right. Lucas hadn't been her Prince Charming and he wasn't ever coming to rescue her. Wherever he had ended up, she imagined it was far from here.

Their first fortnight in Moose River went smoothly. Lily settled in well at her new school. She was thriving and Jess was thrilled. She loved the after-school ski lessons and Jess was looking forward to getting out on the slopes with her this weekend and seeing how much she'd improved in just ten days. It was amazing how quickly children picked up the basics.

She wondered about Lily's fearless attitude. If Lily wanted something she went after it, so different from Jess's reticence. Was that nature or nurture?

Jess had vowed to give Lily freedom—freedom to make her own friends and experience a childhood where she was free to test the boundaries without constant supervision or rules. A childhood without the constant underlying sense that things could, would and did go wrong and where everything had to be micromanaged.

Moose River was, so far, proving to be the perfect place for Lily to have a relaxed childhood and Jess was beginning to feel like she'd made a good decision. Lily had made friends quickly and her new best friend was Annabel, whose parents owned the patisserie next to their apartment building. By the second week the girls had a routine where Lily would go home with Annabel after ski school and have a hot chocolate at the bakery while they waited for Jess to finish work. Jess had been nervous about this at first but she'd reminded herself that this was a benefit of moving to a small community. She'd wanted that sense of belonging. That sense that people would look out for each other. She wanted somewhere where she and Lily would fit in.

Initially she'd felt like they were taking advantage of Annabel's mother but Fleur was adamant that it was no bother. Annabel had two older siblings and Fleur insisted that having Lily around was making life easier for everyone as Annabel was too busy to annoy the others. Jess hated asking for favours, she preferred to feel she could manage by herself even if she knew that wasn't always the case, but she was grateful for Fleur's assistance.

Her new job as a clinic nurse was going just as smoothly as Lily's transition. Her role was easy. She helped with splints, dressings, immunisations and did general health checks—cholesterol, blood pressure and the like. It was routine nursing, nothing challenging, but that suited her. It was low stress and by the end of the two weeks she was feeling confident that coming here had been the right decision for her and Lily.

Not having to work weekends or take extra shifts to cover rent or child-care costs was paying dividends. She could be home with Lily in time for dinner and spend full, uninterrupted days with her over the weekends. It was heaven. Jess adored her daughter and she'd dreamt of being able to spend quality time with her. Just the two of them. It was something she hadn't experienced much in her own childhood and she was determined that Lily would have that quality time with her. After all, they only had each other.

She checked her watch as she tidied her clinic room and got ready to go home. Kristie was coming up for the weekend—in fact, she should already be here. She was changing the sheet on the examination bed when Donna, the practice manager, burst into the room.

'Jess, do you think you could possibly work a little later today? We've had a call from the new hotel, one of their guests is almost thirty-six weeks pregnant and she's having contractions. It might just be Braxton-Hicks but they'd like someone to take a look and all the doctors are busy. Do you think you could go?'

'Let me make some arrangements for Lily and then I'll get over there,' Jess said when Donna finally paused for breath. Jess was happy to go, provided she could sort Lily out. She rang Kristie as she swapped her shoes for boots and explained the situation as she grabbed her coat and the medical bag that Donna had given to her.

Thank God Kristie was in town, she thought as she rang Fleur to tell her of the change in plans. Of course, Fleur then offered to help too but Jess didn't want to push the friendship at this early stage. She explained that Kristie would collect Lily and take her home. She could concentrate on the emergency now. It was always a balancing act, juggling parenting responsibilities with her work, but it seemed she might have the support network here that she'd lacked anywhere else.

Jess hurried the few blocks to Main Street. The five-star, boutique Moose River Crystal Lodge, where her patient was a guest, was the new hotel on the Plaza, the one she'd noticed on the night they'd arrived. She and Lily had walked past it several times since. It was hard to miss. It wasn't huge or ostentatious but it was in a fabulous position, and she'd heard it was beautifully appointed inside.

In the late-afternoon light, the setting sun cast a glow onto the facade of the lodge, making its marble facade

shine a pale silver. On the southern side of the main
entrance was an elevated outdoor seating area, which
would be the perfect spot for an afternoon drink on a
sunny day; you could watch the activities in the plaza
from the perfect vantage point.

A wide footpath connected the lodge to the plaza and
in front of the hotel stood a very placid horse who was
hitched to a smart red wooden sleigh. Lily had begged
to go for a ride when they had walked past earlier in the
week but Jess had fibbed and told her it was for hotel
guests only because she doubted she could afford the
treat. She had meant to find out how much it cost, thinking maybe it could be a Christmas surprise for Lily, but
she had forgotten all about it until now.

She walked past the horse and sleigh and tried to
ignore the feeling of guilt that was so familiar to her
as a single, working mother, struggling to make ends
meet, but walking into the lobby just reinforced how
much her life had changed from one of privilege to one
much harder but she reminded herself it was of her own
choosing.

The lobby was beautifully decorated in dark wood.
Soft, caramel-hued leather couches were grouped
around rich Persian rugs and enormous crystal chan-
deliers hung from the timber ceiling. It looked expensive and luxurious but welcoming. Although it was still
four weeks until Christmas, festive red, green and silver
decorations adorned the room and a wood fire warmed
the restaurant where wide glass doors could open out
onto the outside terrace. Jess tried not to gawk as she
crossed the parquet floor. She'd seen plenty of fancy
hotels but this one had a warmth and a charm about it

that was rare. Maybe because it was small, but it felt more like an exclusive private ski lodge than a hotel.

She shrugged out of her coat as she approached the reception desk.

'I'm Jess Johnson, from the Moose River Medical Centre. Someone called about a woman in labour?'

The young girl behind the desk nodded. 'Yes, Mrs Bertillon. She's in room three zero five on the third floor. I'll just call the hotel manager to take you up.'

'It's okay, I'll find it.' Jess could see the elevators tucked into a short hallway alongside the desk. The hotel was small so she'd have no trouble finding the room. She didn't want to waste time waiting.

She stabbed at the button for the elevator. The doors slid open and she stepped inside.

Jess found room 305 and knocked on the door. It swung open under her hand. There was a bathroom to her left with a wardrobe on the right, forming a short passage. Jess could see a small sofa positioned in front of a large picture window but that was it.

She called out a greeting. 'Mrs Bertillon?'

'Come in.' The faceless voice sounded strong and Jess relaxed. That didn't sound like a woman in labour.

A woman appeared at the end of the passage. She was a hotel employee judging by her uniform. 'She's through here.' The same voice. This wasn't Mrs. Bertillon. 'I'm Margaret. I was keeping an eye on Aimee until you got here,' she explained, and Jess could see the relief on her face. She'd obviously been waiting nervously for reinforcements. 'I'll wait outside now but you can call for me if there's anything you need,' she said, hurriedly abdicating responsibility.

Jess introduced herself to Aimee and got her medical

history as she washed her hands and then wrapped the blood-pressure cuff around her patient's left arm. This was her first pregnancy, Aimee told her, and she'd had no complications. Her blood pressure had been fine, no gestational diabetes, no heart problems. 'I've had some back pain today and now these contractions but otherwise I've been fine.'

'Sharp pain?' asked Jess.

'No. Dull,' Aimee explained, 'more like backache, I suppose. Ow...'

'Is that a contraction now?'

Aimee nodded and Jess looked at her watch, timing the contraction. She could see the contraction ripple across the woman's abdomen as the muscles tightened. This wasn't Braxton-Hicks.

'Your waters haven't broken?' she asked, and Aimee shook her head in reply.

Once the contraction had passed she checked the baby's size and position, pleased to note the baby wasn't breech. But she wasn't so pleased when she discovered that Aimee's cervix was already seven centimetres dilated. Aimee was in labour and there was nothing she could do to stop it.

'Where is your husband?' Jess asked. She'd noticed a wedding ring on Aimee's finger but wondered where Mr Bertillon was.

'He's out skiing,' Aimee replied. 'Why?'

Jess smiled. 'I thought he might like to be here to meet your baby.'

'It's coming now?'

'Mmm-hmm.' Jess nodded. 'You're about to become parents.'

'Oh, my God.'

'Does your husband have a mobile phone with him? Would you like me to call him for you?' Jess asked.

'No. I can do it. I think.' Aimee put a hand on her distended belly as another contraction subsided. 'If I hurry. Jean-Paul will be surprised. This was supposed to be our last holiday before the baby arrived and it wasn't supposed to end like this.' She gave a wry smile. 'Maybe we've been having too much sex. Is it true that can bring on labour?'

Jess couldn't remember the last time she'd had too much sex. She could barely remember the last time she'd had *any* sex. She nodded. 'But not usually at this stage. I think your baby has just decided to join the party.' She concentrated on Aimee. Thinking about sex always made her think about Lucas, especially since she was in Moose River, but now wasn't the time for daydreaming. Aimee needed all her attention.

Aimee's cell phone was beside the bed. Jess passed it to her and then picked up the hotel phone and asked for an ambulance to be sent. Aimee needed to go to the nearest hospital that had premature birthing facilities, which meant leaving Moose River.

Another contraction gripped Aimee and Jess waited as she panted and puffed her way through it. Jess checked her watch. The contractions were two minutes apart. How long would the ambulance take? She had no idea.

Once that contraction had passed and Jess saw Aimee press the buttons on her phone to call her husband she went to gather towels from the bathroom. She stuck her head out into the corridor and asked Margaret to fetch more towels from Housekeeping.

'How did it go? Did you reach Jean-Paul?' Jess asked when she returned to Aimee's side.

'No. It goes straight to his message service.' Aimee gasped and grabbed her belly as another contraction ripped through her. 'He's gone skiing with a snowcat group so I can only assume he's out in the wilderness and out of range.'

Margaret came into the room with an armful of towels and Jess asked if there was any way of getting a message to Jean-Paul.

'Yes, of course,' Margaret replied. 'Will you be all right on your own with Aimee while I organise that?'

Jess nodded. Margaret wasn't going to be of any further use. It was the ambos Jess wanted to see. Jess tucked several of the towels underneath Aimee. She knew it was probably a futile exercise but if Aimee's waters broke she was hoping to limit the damage to the hotel bedding. Another contraction gripped Aimee and this one was accompanied by a gush of fluid. Fortunately it wasn't a big flood and Jess suspected that meant the baby's head was well down into Aimee's pelvis.

Jess used the time between contractions to check Aimee's cervix. Eight centimetres dilated. This was really happening. If the ambos didn't hurry she would have to deliver the baby. What would she need?

She'd need to keep the baby warm. She put a couple of the clean towels back on the heated towel rail in the bathroom.

Aimee's cries were getting louder and she had a sheen of perspiration across her forehead. 'I want to push,' she called out.

'Hang on,' Jess cautioned, and she checked progress again.

Oh no. The baby's head was crowning already.

Jess felt for the cord. It felt loose and she just hoped it wasn't around the baby's neck.

'Okay, Aimee. This is it. You can push with the next contraction.'

Jess saw the contraction ripple across Aimee's skin. 'Okay, bend your knees and push!'

The baby's head appeared and Jess was able to turn the baby to deliver one shoulder with the next contraction and the baby slid into her hands. 'It's a girl,' she told Aimee. Jess rubbed the baby's back, checking to make sure her little chest rose and fell with a breath and listening for her first cry before she placed her on Aimee's chest and fetched a warm towel. She took one-minute Apgar readings and clamped the cord just as the ambos arrived. Relief flooded through her. She'd done the easy bit, now they could finish off.

'Congratulations, Aimee.'

'Thank you.' Aimee's smile was gentle but she barely lifted her eyes from her baby. She was oblivious to the work the ambos were doing. Nothing could distract her from the miracle of new life.

Jess could remember that feeling, that vague, blissful state of euphoria. She tidied her things, packing them into her bag as she thought about Lily's birth. Like Aimee, she'd done it without the baby's father there.

She hadn't wanted to do it alone but she hadn't had a lot of choice. She hadn't expected their relationship to end so suddenly. She hadn't expected a lot of things.

By the time she'd discovered she was pregnant the ski fields had closed for the season and Lily's father had been long gone, and despite her best efforts she hadn't been able to find him. So she'd done it alone and she'd done her best.

She snapped her medical bag closed with shaky hands. Now that the drama was over her body shook with the adrenalin that coursed through her system. She stripped the bed as the ambos transferred Aimee and her baby onto a stretcher and wheeled them out the door.

She could hear voices in the hallway and assumed that Jean-Paul had been located. That was quick. She could hear an Australian accent too. That was odd. Jean-Paul didn't sound like an Australian name. She listened more carefully.

A male voice, an Australian accent. It sounded a lot like Lucas.

Her stomach flipped and her heart began to race. She was being ridiculous. It had been seven years since she'd heard his voice, as if she'd remember exactly how he sounded. She only imagined it was him because he'd been in her thoughts.

It wouldn't be him. It couldn't be him.

But she couldn't resist taking a look.

She picked up the medical bag and stepped out into the hallway. The ambos had halted the stretcher and a man stood with his back to her, talking to Aimee.

'We've got a message to your husband,' he was saying. 'We'll get him back as quickly as possible and I'll make sure he gets brought to the hospital.'

The man was tall with broad shoulders and tousled blond hair. Jess could see narrow hips and long, lean legs. His voice was deep with a sexy Aussie drawl. Her heart beat quickened, pumping the blood around her body, leaving her feeling light-headed and faint.

It was him. It was most definitely him.

She steadied herself with one hand against the wall as she prayed that her knees wouldn't buckle.

It was Lucas.

She didn't need to see his face. She knew it and her body knew it. Every one of her cells was straining towards him. Seven years may have passed but her body hadn't forgotten him and neither had she. She recognised the length of his legs, the shape of his backside, the sound of his voice.

The ambos were pushing the stretcher towards the elevator by the time she found her voice.

'Lucas?'

CHAPTER THREE

JESS FELT AS if the ground was tipping beneath her feet. She felt as if at any moment she might slide to the floor. She could see the scene playing out in front of her, almost as though she was a spectator watching from the sidelines. She could see herself wobbling in the foreground and she could see Lucas standing close enough to touch. If she could just reach out a hand she could feel him. See if he really was real. But she couldn't move. Life seemed to be going on around her as she watched, too overcome to react.

He turned towards her at the sound of his name.

'JJ?'

She hadn't been called JJ in years. It had been his nickname for her and no one else had ever used it.

She couldn't believe he was standing in front of her. Lucas, undeniably Lucas. He still had the same brilliant, forget-me-not-blue eyes and the same infectious, dimpled smile and he was smiling now as he stepped forward and wrapped her in a hug. She fitted perfectly into his embrace and it felt like it was only yesterday that she'd last been in his arms. Memories flooded back to her and her stomach did a peculiar little flip as her body responded in a way it hadn't for years. She tensed, taken by surprise by both his spontaneous gesture and her reaction.

He must have felt her stiffen because he let her go and stepped away.

Her eyes took in the sight of him. He looked fabulous. The years had been kind to him. Better than they'd been to her, she feared. His hair was cut shorter but was still sandy blond and thick, and his oval face was tanned, making his blue eyes even more striking. He had the shadow of a beard on his jaw, more brown than blond. That was new. He wouldn't have had that seven years ago, but he hadn't got fat. Or bald.

Her heart raced as she looked him over. He was wearing dark trousers and a pale blue business shirt. It was unbuttoned at the collar, no tie, and he had his sleeves rolled up to expose his forearms. He looked just as good, maybe even better, than she remembered.

Her initial surprise was immediately followed by pleasure but that was then, just as quickly, cancelled out by panic. What was he doing here? He wasn't supposed to be here. He was supposed to be in Europe or Australia. Eating cheese in Switzerland or surfing at Bondi Beach. He wasn't supposed to be in Canada and especially not in Moose River. *She* was the one who belonged here. *She* was the Canadian.

'What are you doing here?' she asked him.

'I'm the hotel manager.'

'In Moose River?'

'It would seem so.' He grinned at her and her stomach did another flip as heat seared through her, scorching her insides. He didn't seem nearly as unsettled as she was about their unexpected encounter. But, then, he'd always adapted quickly to new situations. He seemed to thrive on change, whereas she would rather avoid it.

The ambos and Aimee and her baby had disappeared and a second elevator pinged as it reached their floor.

'Are you finished up here?' he asked.

Jess nodded. It seemed she'd lost the power of speech. It seemed as though Lucas had the same effect on her now as he'd had seven years ago.

'I'll ride down with you,' he said.

He waited for her to enter the elevator. She tucked herself into the corner by the door, feeling confused. Conflicted. She wasn't sure what to think. She wasn't sure how she felt. One part of her wanted to throw herself into his arms and never let him go. Another wanted to run and hide. Another wanted desperately to know what he was thinking.

Lucas stepped in and reached across in front of her to press the button to take them down to the lobby. She hadn't remembered to push the button, so distracted by him she wasn't thinking clearly.

He was standing close. She'd expected him to lean against the opposite wall but he didn't move away as the elevator descended. If she reached out a hand she could touch him without even straightening her elbow.

He was watching her with his forget-me-not-blue eyes and she couldn't take her eyes off him. His familiar scent washed over her—he smelt like winter in the mountains, cool and crisp with the clean, fresh tang of pine needles.

The air was humming, drowning out the silence that fell between them. She clenched her fists at her sides to stop herself from reaching out. She could feel herself being pulled towards him. Even after all this time her body longed for his touch. She craved him.

They stood, for what seemed like ages, just looking at each other.

'It's good to see you, JJ.' His voice was a whisper, barely breaking the silence that surrounded them.

He stretched out one hand and Jess held her breath. His fingers caught the ends of her hair and his thumb brushed across her cheek. The contact set her nerves on fire, every inch of her responding to his touch. It felt like every one of her cells had a memory and every memory was Lucas.

'You've cut your hair,' he said.

'Many times,' she replied.

Lucas laughed and the sound was loud enough to burst the bubble of awareness and desire and longing that had enveloped her.

She didn't know how she'd managed to make a joke. Nothing about this was funny. She was so ill prepared to run into him.

Last time he'd seen her she'd had long hair that had fallen past her shoulders. She'd cut it short when Lily had been born and now it was softly feathered and the ends brushed her shoulders. She'd changed many things about herself since he'd last seen her, not just her hair. It was almost a surprise that he'd recognised her. She felt seventy years older. Not seven. Like a completely different person.

She *was* a different person.

She was a mother. A mother with a secret.

The lift doors slid open but Jess didn't move. Lucas was in her way but even so she didn't think she was capable of movement. She needed the wall to support her.

Her legs were shaking. Her hands were shaking. She knew her reaction was a result of the adrenalin that was coursing through her system. Adrenalin that was produced from a combination of attraction and fear. Why had he come back? And what would his presence mean to her? And to Lily?

'Mr White.' A hotel staff member approached them. Lucas had his back to the doors but he turned at the sound of his name and stepped out of the elevator. 'Mr Bertillon is nearly back at the lodge. He's only a minute or two away. What would you like me to do?'

'I'll meet him here. Can you organise a car to be waiting out the front? We need to get him down the mountain to the hospital asap.'

Jess pushed off the wall and forced her legs to move. One step at a time, she could do this. Lucas turned back to face her as she stepped into the lobby. 'Have you got time for a coffee? Can you wait while I sort this out?'

Jess shook her head. 'I have to get back to the medical centre,' she lied. She had no idea how to deal with the situation. With Lucas. She had to get away. She needed time to process what had just happened. To process the fact that Lucas was here.

'Of course. Another time, then.' He put a hand on her arm and it felt as though her skin might burst into flames at his touch. Her pulse throbbed. Her throat was dry. 'We'll catch up later,' he said.

Jess dropped the medical bag off at the clinic before trudging through the snow back to her apartment. Seeing Lucas had left her shaky and confused and she used the few minutes she had to herself to try to sort out her feelings.

He said they'd catch up later. What would he want?

She definitely wasn't the naive teenager from seven years ago. She wasn't the person he would remember.

What would she do? She needed to work out what to tell him. How to tell him.

She shook her head. This was all too much.

She'd have to try to avoid him. Just for a while, just until she worked out what having all three of them in the same place would mean for her and Lily. Just until she solved this dilemma.

Seven years ago she'd fallen in love. Or she'd thought she had. Seven years on she had convinced herself that maybe it had just been a bad case of teenage hormones. Lust. A holiday romance. But seeing him today had reinforced that she'd never got over him. How could she when she was reminded of him every day?

She knew she wouldn't be able to avoid him for ever. Moose River wasn't big enough for that. They were bound to bump into each other. But even if avoidance was a possibility she suspected she wouldn't be able to resist him completely. Curiosity would get the better of her. She'd been thinking about him for seven years. She would have to fill in the gaps. But as to exactly what she would tell him, that decision could wait.

She opened her apartment door and was almost knocked over by an excited Lily.

'Mum, where have you been? Kristie is here. We've been waiting for you for ages.'

'Yes, darling, I know. I'm sorry I'm late,' she said as she kissed her daughter.

Normally, seeing Lily's little face light up when she arrived home after a long day at work was enough to lift her spirits. Normally, it was enough to remind her of why she worked so hard and why she'd made the choices she had, but today all she could think of was all the secrets she had kept and wonder how much longer she had until the secrets came out.

She felt ill. The living room was warm but she was shivering. Trembling, Kristie got up and hugged her and Jess could feel herself shaking against her cousin's shoulder.

Kristie stepped back and looked at Jess while she spoke to Lily. 'Lily, why don't you go and try on that new skisuit I got for you? I think your mum would like to see it.' She waited for Lily to leave the room and then said to Jess. 'What's going on? Did it go badly with the patient?'

'No, that was all fine,' Jess replied. She'd been going to stop there but she knew Kristie would get the news out of her eventually. She'd always known when something was bothering her and she'd always been able to wheedle it out of her. She decided she may as well come clean now. 'It's Lucas.'

'What do you mean, "It's Lucas"? What's he got to do with anything?'

Jess collapsed onto the couch. 'He's not in Switzerland or on Bondi Beach. He's here.'

'Here? In Moose River?'

'Yes.'

'What's he doing here?' Kristie sat down opposite Jess.

'He's managing the Crystal Lodge.'

'The new hotel? How did you find that out?' she asked, when Jess nodded.

'I saw him there.'

'You've seen him?'

She nodded again.

'Oh, my God! What did he say? How did he look? What did *you* say?'

'Not much. Good. Nothing.' She couldn't remember what she'd said. All she could remember was how he'd looked and how she'd felt. How those eyes had made her catch her breath, how her knees had turned to jelly when he'd smiled, how her heart had raced when he'd said her name, and how he'd wrapped her in his arms and she'd never wanted to leave. How, after all these years, she still fitted perfectly in his embrace.

'Look, Mum, it's pink.' Jess jumped as her reverie was interrupted by Lily modelling her new skisuit. 'Isn't it pretty?'

'It's very nice, darling,' she replied, without really looking at her mini-fashionista. She was finding it hard to focus on anything other than Lucas. 'Now, why don't you get ready for a bath while I do something about dinner.'

Lily stamped her foot. 'I want to stay in my suit and I don't want dinner.'

'You need to eat something and you don't want to get your new suit dirty, do you?'

Lily folded her arms across her chest and scowled at her mother. 'I don't want dinner.'

'I bought Lily a burger and fries after school. She won't be going to bed hungry,' Kristie said.

'She ate it?'

'She ate the fries and about half the burger.'

Jess was pleased. Maybe the fresh mountain air was stimulating her appetite. Maybe a compromise could be reached.

'Okay, you don't need to eat but you do need to have a bath and put your pyjamas on. Then you can hop into bed, put the headphones on and watch a movie on the laptop.'

That was a bribe and a compromise but it worked. Lily thought she was getting a treat and she stopped complaining. It worked for Jess too as it meant she and Kristie could talk without fear of being overheard. She knew Kristie would continue to pump her for information and she didn't want to discuss Lucas in front of Lily.

By the time Jess had bathed Lily and got her settled with her movie Kristie had ordered a pizza and poured them both a glass of wine. The moment Jess emerged from the bedroom she could tell she was in for a grilling.

'What are you going to do?' Kristie asked, as Jess drew the curtains on the balcony doors and shut out the night.

'Nothing.'

'You can't do nothing! He deserves to know.'

'Why? My father was right. Obviously the week we spent together didn't mean as much to him as it did to me. If Lucas wanted to be a part of my life he's had plenty of time to look for me before now.'

'You know you don't believe that,' Kristie said. 'You didn't believe your father seven years ago and you don't believe that now. If we could have found Lucas all those years ago he'd be part of your life already.'

'But we couldn't find him and my life is fine as it is,' she argued.

'But what about Lily? Doesn't she deserve to know?'

Jess greeted Kristie's question with stony silence.

'You can't put off the inevitable,' Kristie added. 'It's not fair to Lucas and it's not fair to Lily.'

'But I have no idea what type of man he is now,' Jess countered. He might not be the person she remembered. *Did* she even remember him? Maybe everything she remembered had been a product of her imagination but she knew one thing for certain—she wasn't the person he would remember.

She'd dreamt of Lucas coming back into her life but now that he was here she was nervous. His return brought complications she hadn't considered and consequences she wasn't ready for. She wasn't ready to deal with having him back in her life. She rolled her eyes at herself. Who said he would even want to be part of her life? Or Lily's? This wasn't a fairy tale. This was reality.

She sighed. One thing at a time. That was how she would deal with this. She would gather the facts and then work out her approach, and until then she would stay as far away from him as possible.

'I need some answers before I tell him anything,' she said.

'You can't avoid him for ever.'

'I just need some time to process this,' she said. No matter how much she'd wished for one more chance, now that the moment was here she wasn't ready. 'Whatever we had was over a long time ago. It was a teenage romance—it's water under the bridge now.'

'It might be,' Kristie argued, 'except for the fact that the bridge is sleeping in the other room. There's always going to be something connecting you to him.'

And Jess knew that was the crux of the matter.

Lily.

'You can't keep her a secret any more, Jess.'

CHAPTER FOUR

IT TOOK A lot to frustrate Lucas. He was normally a calm person, level-headed and patient, all good attributes when working in hospitality, but right now he was frustrated. Seeing Jess again had hit him for six. It was a cricketing term but one that perfectly matched how he was feeling. He could cope with the day-to-day issues that arose with the hotel, he'd even coped with the delays and revisions while it had been redeveloped, but he couldn't cope with Jess's disappearance. Not again.

By the time he'd waited for Aimee Bertillon's husband and seen the ambulance off, all the while itching to return to Jess but doing his best to hide his impatience, she had vanished. She had said she couldn't wait and it seemed she'd meant it.

He knew he wouldn't be able to settle, he wouldn't be able to concentrate on work, not while thoughts of Jess were running rampant through his head. He told his PA that he was going out. No excuses, no reasons. He needed to think and he always thought better if he was outside in the fresh air. If she wasn't going to wait for him, he'd go and find her. He changed his shoes and grabbed his coat and walked to the medical centre.

'Can I help you?' The lady behind the desk had a
name badge that read 'Donna'.

'I hope so. I'm looking for one of your doctors, Jess
Johnson.'

'She's not a doctor,' Donna told him.

Now he was confused as well as frustrated. 'I've just
seen her. I'm Lucas White from the Crystal Lodge. I
called for a doctor and she came.'

'Jess is a nurse. All our doctors were busy so she
agreed to go and make an assessment. Was there a problem? She's gone for the day but is there something I can
help you with?'

A nurse.

Lucas shook his head. 'No. Nothing. Thank you.'
The only thing he wanted was to know where she was
and he didn't imagine that Donna would give him that
information. He'd have to come back.

Jess was a nurse. He wondered what had happened.
She'd been planning on becoming a doctor—why hadn't
she followed her dream?

Night had fallen when he stepped back outside and
the temperature had dropped. He pulled his scarf and
gloves out of his coat pocket—he'd learnt years ago to
keep them handy—and wandered the streets, still hoping to find her.

If he'd known on the day she'd been yanked from his
life that he wasn't ever going to see her again he would
have tried harder to keep hold of her. When she'd disappeared he'd been left with nothing. Nothing but a sense
that he needed to prove himself.

He had left Moose River to return home, vowing he
would make it back one day. Vowing to make something
of himself. For her. It had been an impulsive, young

man's promise, one that seven years later he might have thought would be long forgotten, but even though there had been plenty of other women over the years he'd never got Jess out of his system. She'd been an irresistible combination of beauty, brains, innocence and passion. She had worn her heart on her sleeve and she'd shared herself with him without reservation.

At times it was almost impossible to believe they'd only had seven days together. That one week had influenced him profoundly. It had made him the man he was today, determined to succeed. Determined to find Jess again and prove himself worthy.

It had taken longer than he would have dreamed. If someone had told him at the age of twenty that it would take him almost seven years, he would have thought that was a whole lifetime. But he had done it and he was back.

When the opportunity had presented itself in Moose River he'd jumped at it. At the time it had seemed as though all the planets had aligned. The timing had been right, he'd been ready to spread his wings, and the opportunity to be back in Moose River had been too good a chance to pass up. He'd wanted to prove himself and what better place to do it than in the very place where his dreams had all begun.

He'd returned as a successful, self-made man but things hadn't gone quite as he'd expected. The hotel hadn't been the problem. It had been Jess. He'd been back in Moose River for nine months and hadn't caught sight of her until today. He hadn't imagined that he'd find her, only to have her disappear again. Maybe she didn't feel the same desire to catch up. Maybe she hadn't kept hold of the memories, as he had. Maybe she barely remembered him.

Although he'd seen in her face that she hadn't forgotten him. He'd held her in his arms and it had felt like yesterday and he knew she'd felt it too.

But things had not gone according to his plan. The reunion he'd always pictured had gone quite differently.

But he wasn't a quitter, he never had been, and he wasn't about to start now. He'd found her and he wasn't going to let her disappear again.

He walked past the building where Jess's family had had their apartment all those years ago. He'd called in there before but this time he knew she was in town. She had to be staying somewhere. He pushed open the lobby door and pressed the buzzer for the penthouse.

No answer. That would have been far too easy.

He continued walking and eventually stopped and leant on a lamppost. He looked across the street and recognised the building. He was in front of the Moose River staff apartments. He counted the windows and stopped at unit fifteen. It was in darkness but he could see lights in the gap between the curtains in apartment sixteen. His gaze drifted back to the dark windows of fifteen as his memory wandered.

Jess had given him her heart but he hadn't really appreciated it at the time. He'd been young and hungry for adventure. He hadn't realised what he'd had with her. Not until she'd been long gone. And by then it had been too late.

No one else had ever measured up to her. Or not to his idealisation of her anyway. Perhaps he was looking back on the past with rose-tinted glasses but there had been something special about her and he'd never met anyone else like her. And he'd travelled to almost every corner of the globe. He'd been constantly on the go since he'd left Moose River. He'd immersed himself in the hospitality trade before he'd even finished studying, learning the lessons that enabled him to take the next step, getting the knowledge and experience to embark on a solo project. Getting ready to prove himself to Jess and her father.

But he wasn't to know his efforts were to be in vain.

Apartment fifteen remained dark. He wasn't going to solve the puzzle that was life or even the problem that was Jess and her whereabouts while standing out here in the cold. There were plenty of issues waiting for his attention back at the lodge. He could make better use of his time. He pushed off the lamppost and trudged back through the snow. He'd continue to search for her tomorrow.

Lucas had been up since five. He'd been unable to sleep and he'd done half a day's work already. It was Thanksgiving weekend in the United States and the official start of the ski season in Moose River, Canada. Crowds were building and the Crystal Lodge was fully booked. This was what he'd wanted. What he'd been working towards. No vacancies. He wanted Crystal Lodge to become one of the premier hotels in the resort. But now he feared that wasn't enough. Jess was back and he wanted her too.

He loved his job, he loved his life and he'd thought that he was happy with his success, but seeing Jess yesterday had shown him that all his success was nothing if he had no one to share it with. Seeing her yesterday reinforced that he'd spent seven years making something of himself, of his life, and he'd done it for her. But had she moved on? What would be the point of making himself worthy of Jess if she didn't want to have anything to do with him?

He stood by the window of his office and watched the snow fall. It had started early this morning and the forecast was for heavy falls over the weekend. It was perfect for the start of the season.

Next week all the Christmas decorations would be up around the village. They were already multiplying at a rapid rate and Lucas knew his tradesmen were at work this morning, building a frame for the thirty-foot tree that would be on display in front of the hotel on the plaza. He planned to switch on the lights on the tree next weekend to coincide with the opening of the Christmas market that was to be held in the plaza. There were plenty of things needing his attention, he had plenty to keep him occupied, but all he could think about was Jess.

He needed a break from the indoors. He muttered something to his PA about inspecting the progress on the framework for the tree and then wandered through the village, retracing his steps to all the places he and Jess had spent time seven years ago. Not that he expected to find her in the same places but he was happy to let his feet lead the way as it left his mind free to reminisce.

He headed up the hill, past the popular après-ski venue, the T-bar, and skirted the iconic Moose River Hotel, which set the standard for accommodation and was the hotel that Lucas measured the performance of Crystal Lodge against. The village was blanketed in snow. It was as pretty as a picture but everyone was bundled up against the weather and he knew he could walk right past Jess and never know it. He may as well return to the lodge and do something more productive.

He was halfway down the hill, passing the tube park, when he spotted her. She was leaning on the railing at the bottom of the slope and he could see her profile as she watched people sliding down the hill in the inflatable rubber tubes. She was wearing a red knitted cap and he had a flashback to the day he'd first met her. How the hell did he remember that? The sound of laughter floated up to him as people raced down the lanes and Lucas felt like laughing along with them. He'd found her.

'JJ!'

Jess turned around at the sound of her nickname. Her heart was racing even before she saw him. Just hearing his voice was enough to make her feel like she was seventeen once more and falling in love all over again. He was smiling at her and she couldn't help but smile back, even as she cursed her heart for betraying her brain.

'I was hoping to bump into you.'

That was ironic. She'd been hoping to avoid him.

'You were? What for?'

'Old times' sake. I wanted to invite you for coffee. Or dinner?'

'I don't think so,' Jess replied. She was nowhere near ready to spend one-on-one time with Lucas. She knew she owed it to him to catch up but she wasn't ready yet. She needed time to prepare. She needed time to plan a defence. And she definitely needed more than twenty-four hours.

'Jess!'

Kristie was flying down the slope towards them in a double tube. The snow had been falling too heavily to make for pleasant skiing with a beginner so she and Kristie had opted to bring Lily to the tube park instead. But she hadn't anticipated that they'd bump into Lucas. Not here.

She used the interruption to her advantage, choosing to wave madly at her cousin and hoping to divert Lucas's attention.

'Is that Kristie?'

'Yes.' Kristie had Lily tucked between her knees and she was screaming at the top of her lungs as they raced alongside the person in the adjacent lane. Kristie always took things to the extreme and Lily was yelling right along with her, looking like she was having the time of her life.

Jess could remember coming to the tube park with Lucas. She could remember sitting in the tube between his thighs with his arms wrapped around her and yelling with delight, just like Lily was now. Life had been so much simpler then but she hadn't appreciated it at the time.

'Who's that with her?' Lucas asked, as he spotted Lily.

Jess had successfully diverted Lucas's attention away from herself, only to focus it on Lily. The one thing she didn't want.

She was tempted to tell him that Lily was Kristie's but she knew she'd be caught out far too easily in that lie. 'That's my daughter,' she said.

'You have a daughter?'

Kristie and Lily hopped out of the tube and Kristie started dragging it back to the conveyor belt that would take them back to the start of the lanes at the top of the hill. Lily waved to Jess but followed Kristie. Luckily, she wasn't ready for the fun to end yet so didn't come over to her mother. Jess was relieved. She didn't want to have to introduce Lily to Lucas. Not yet. She definitely wasn't prepared for that.

'She's the image of you,' Lucas said, as Lily stepped onto the conveyor belt. 'How old is she?'

'Five.' Jess's heart was beating at a million miles an hour as she avoided one lie only to tell another.

Lily was, in fact, six, but luckily she was small for her age. While Jess didn't want to give Lucas a chance to put two and two together, she wasn't completely certain why she'd lied. She didn't expect him to remember that it had been seven years ago that they had spent one week together. It was obvious he hadn't forgotten her but to think he would remember exactly how many years had passed might be stretching things. Just because that time had become so significant to Jess, it didn't mean it would be as important to him. Why should it be? It had been just one week for him. For her it had been the rest of her life.

'Is that the reason you don't want to catch up? You're married?'

Jess shook her head. 'No.'

'Divorced?'

'No, but I still can't go to dinner with you. Life is more complicated now.' She had to think of Lily. But she knew she was also thinking of herself. She wasn't ready for this.

'I guess it is.' He nodded his head slowly as he absorbed her words. 'But, if you do find yourself free at any time, or if your complications become less complicated, you know where to contact me.'

He didn't push her. He didn't suggest she bring Lily

along to dinner and Jess knew he wanted to see only her. Alone.

Was it possible that her father had been right? If she'd been able to find Lucas all those years ago would he have wanted to know about Lily or would he have chosen to have nothing to do with her? She didn't think that was the sort of person he was. But what would she know? It wasn't like they'd had time to really get to know each other.

She wondered if he'd ever thought about being a father. Maybe he already was one. The question was on the tip of her tongue but she bit it back. Did she want to know more about him? Did she want to know what his life was like now? What if he had children of his own? Other children? Would that be too painful?

Surely it was better, safer, easier if she kept her distance.

He smiled. His forget-me-not-blue eyes were shining and his dimples flashed briefly, tempting her to say, *Wait, yes, of course I'd love to have dinner with you.* But she nodded and let him go.

She watched him walk down the hill and thought about how different her life could have been.

Jess stood at the balcony doors as the last rays of the sun dipped behind the mountain. She had thought that spending the morning at the tube park would have exhausted Lily but she seemed full of beans and Jess didn't have the energy to cope with her at the moment. Thank goodness for Kristie. She had taken Lily off to the shops, leaving Jess alone to think.

She looked to her left, down to the village. In the foreground she could see the balcony of apartment fifteen,

Lucas's old apartment. She tried to look past it as she
didn't want to think about him but she knew she couldn't
help it. Her mind had been filled with memories of him
all day and right there, on that balcony, was where they
had shared their first kiss.

When Lucas and Sam had invited them to their party
Jess had never imagined actually going. But Kristie had
managed to come up with a semi-believable story about
a school friend's birthday and before she'd known it Jess
had been at Lucas's door.

He and Sam had been sharing the apartment with
two other boys and it had already been crowded when
they'd arrived. People had spilled out of the living room
into the corridor between the flats, overflowing into the
bedrooms and out onto the balcony. But somehow Lucas
had met her and Kristie at his front door.

He'd smiled at her and his blue eyes had lit up. His
grin had been infectious and full of cheek and Jess had
known right then that he would love creating mischief
and mayhem. 'You look great,' he told her.

She and Kristie had spent ages getting ready, all the
while ensuring that it had looked effortless. Kristie had
straightened Jess's hair so that it hung in a shiny, platinum cascade down her back. She had coated her eyelashes with mascara to highlight her green eyes and
swiped pink gloss over her lips.

She'd been nervous about coming to the party, worried about being in a room full of strangers, but one
smile from Lucas and all her nervousness had disappeared. He hadn't felt like a stranger. She'd felt safe
with him. She'd trusted him. All those years of listening to her parents telling her to be wary of strangers, of
forbidding her to go out alone, and what had she done

at the first opportunity—she'd disappeared to a party with a stranger just because he'd been cute and he'd flirted with her. He'd been so gorgeous and she'd been pretty sure she was already in trouble but she'd been unable to resist.

Even Kristie couldn't have predicted this turnaround in such a short time. Jess, who'd never gone against her parents' wishes, had been rebelling big time because a cute boy had smiled at her and made her laugh. She hadn't known him but she hadn't cared. She would get to know him. She'd felt like she'd been where she was supposed to be. Here. With him.

He took the drinks they carried, opened one for each of them and handed them back before stashing the rest into a tub that had been filled with snow. Kristie had used a fake ID to buy the pre-mixed cans of vodka and soda and they'd shared one as they'd walked to the party. Jess had needed it for courage; she hadn't really planned on having another one but she supposed she could nurse one drink for the evening. It's not like anyone would pay attention to what she was doing.

'I'm glad you could make it,' he said to her, as Kristie spotted Sam and made a beeline for him.

'We almost didn't.'

'How come?'

'We're not normally allowed to go to random parties.'

'Who would stop you?'

'Our parents.'

'So you're not nineteen, then?'

Jess frowned. What did her age have to do with anything? 'What?'

'If you were nineteen you'd be making your own decisions.'

They'd fibbed to her aunt and uncle about where they were going but she'd forgotten that Kristie had also lied to the boys about their age.

'I'll be eighteen next week.' She hoped that wouldn't matter. She wasn't sure what she wanted to happen but she wanted a chance to find out. She didn't want Lucas to decide she was too young but he didn't mention her age again.

'So you've sneaked out and no one knows where you are. Are you sure that's wise?'

'You seemed trustworthy.' Jess smiled. 'And as long as we're home before midnight, everything should be fine,' she added, aware that she was babbling. Normally if she was nervous she'd be tongue-tied but she had forgotten to be nervous. Was it the half a drink she'd had or was there something about Lucas that made her feel comfortable?

'What trouble can you get into after midnight that you can't get into before?' he asked.

'You sound like Kristie.'

'You have to admit I have a point.' Lucas was standing very close to her. When had he closed the distance? She was leaning with her back against a wall and he was standing at a right angle to her, his left shoulder pressed against the same wall, inches away from her. His voice was quiet and he had a mischievous look in his blue eyes.

'I don't know the answer,' she said. 'I just know we need to be home before our curfew. I don't want anyone looking for us and finding out we're not where we said we'd be. I don't tend to get into trouble.'

'Not ever?' He grinned at her and suddenly Jess could imagine all sorts of trouble she could get into.

Trouble, mischief and mayhem. All sorts of things she'd never exposed herself to before.

She shook her head. 'I've never had the opportunity.'

Her parents knew where she was every minute of the day and Jess knew how stressed they would be if she ever sneaked off and went against their wishes. She had never wanted to test the boundaries before, aware of how upset they would be. But neither they nor her aunt and uncle had any idea where she was tonight. If she was careful she could have some fun and they would be none the wiser.

'Maybe you just haven't recognised opportunity when she's come knocking,' Lucas said. 'Or maybe you need to create it.'

His last sentence was barely a whisper. His head was bent close to hers and she held her breath as he dipped his head a little lower. He was going to kiss her! She closed her eyes and leant towards him.

'Hey, Lucas,' someone interrupted. 'Your shout.'

'You've gotta be kidding me.' He lifted his head and turned to face the room. Over his shoulder Jess could see a couple of his mates holding empty beer bottles up in the air and laughing, and she knew they'd deliberately interrupted the moment. Jess could have screamed with frustration. She'd never forgive them if she'd missed an opportunity that she couldn't get back. What if the moment was gone for ever?

'Come on.' He took her by the hand and her skin burned where his fingers wrapped around hers. He pushed through the crowd until they came to a pair of doors that opened onto a balcony. He led her outside to where there were more tubs filled with snow and beers.

He let her go as he grabbed a couple of beers in each hand and asked, 'Will you wait here?'

She wasn't sure what she was waiting for but she nodded anyway. She seemed destined to follow his lead. Something about him made her finally understand what got Kristie all hot and bothered when it came to boys. Her hormones were going into overdrive and she was certain she could still feel the imprint of his fingers on hers. She couldn't think about anything except what it would be like to be kissed by Lucas. He was cute and confident, his accent was completely sexy and the way he looked at her with those brilliant blue eyes made her want to leap in, even though she didn't have the faintest idea about how to do that. But she suspected he knew what to do and she would happily let him teach her.

He took the beers inside and when he came back to her he was holding two coats and another drink for her that she didn't really want. He handed her the can, not realising she hadn't finished her first drink.

'You're not having anything?' she asked.

'I don't feel like drinking tonight.'

He was looking at her so intensely that even with her limited experience Jess knew exactly what he did feel like doing and the idea took her breath away.

'I don't want this either,' she said.

Lucas reached out and closed his hand around hers. It was warm, really warm in contrast to the cold drink. He took the can from her and stuck it into a tub with the beers.

Lucas was making Jess feel light-headed and giddy and she didn't want alcohol to interfere with her senses. She wanted to remember this moment, how it made her feel. She finally felt as if the world made sense.

She had always believed in love at first sight. She didn't know why, but she liked the idea that people could recognise their soul mate the very first time they saw them and she imagined that this was how it would feel. Like you couldn't breathe but you didn't need to. She felt as if she could exist just by looking into Lucas's eyes. She felt as though she didn't need anything more than that. Ever.

'I thought we could stay out here,' he said. 'There'll be fewer interruptions and, you never know, we might find the only thing that interrupts us is opportunity.' He was standing only inches from her. She could see his breath coming from between his lips as little puffs of condensation that accompanied his words and it was only then she noticed the cold. He opened one of the coats and held it for her as she slipped her arms into the sleeves. It smelt like him, fresh and clean with a hint of pine needles, but it swamped her tiny frame.

'How long are you staying at the resort?' he asked, as he rolled the sleeves up for her. He had closed the balcony doors and while they could still see the party through the glass the music was muted and they had the balcony to themselves.

'A little over two weeks. Until the New Year.'

'Do you come here often?'

'We spend most Christmas vacations here.' That was true of the past nine years. Prior to that, when her brother had been alive, they'd spent every second Christmas in California with her mother's family. But that had all changed after Stephen had died. But she didn't think Lucas needed to hear that story. Tonight wasn't about her family. It wasn't about her past. Tonight was about her. Tonight was her chance to experience all the things that Stephen's early death had robbed her of.

'Christmas in the snow,' he said. 'I'm looking forward to seeing what all the fuss is about. This will be my first white Christmas.'

'Really?'

He nodded.

'I'll have to make sure you get the full festive season experience, then,' Jess said with a smile. She'd worry about how to actually achieve that later.

'Don't worry, I intend to.'

He was watching her closely and she started to wonder if she had food caught between her teeth. Why else would he be staring at her like that? 'What is it?' she asked.

'I want to know what you're thinking,' he told her.

'About what?'

'About me.'

She hesitated before answering. She could hardly tell him she thought he was gorgeous or that he might well be her soul mate. He might appreciate her honesty but then again he might think she was completely crazy. She played it safe. 'I don't know anything about you.'

'What would you like to know?'

'I have no idea.' She wasn't very good at social conversations. She'd never really had to talk to a stranger before. She usually only got to talk to people with whom she already had some sort of connection—family, school friends or family friends. There was never anything new to learn about any of them. Every one of them was the same. Rich, well educated and well spoken, they all lived in Vancouver's exclusive suburbs, had private school educations, holiday homes, overseas vacations and were gifted new cars on their sixteenth birthdays. She was surrounded by trust-fund children. Lucas was a clean slate and she didn't know where to begin.

'Well, why don't I start?' he said.

'All right.'

'Do you have a boyfriend?'

She shook her head. 'No. Why?'

'I want to kiss you and I want to know if that's okay.'

Jess's green eyes opened wide. He was offering her a chance to experience freedom. To do something spontaneous, something that hadn't been sanctioned by her parents.

She'd broken so many rules tonight, what was one more? And, besides, there wasn't actually a rule forbidding her to kiss boys. It was more that she was rarely given the opportunity. And that was what it was all about, wasn't it? Opportunity.

Her freedom in Moose River was on borrowed time and if she didn't grab the opportunity with both hands now she knew she'd miss it altogether. She didn't have time to stop and think. She didn't have time to weigh up the options and the pros and cons. Her time was finite. It was now or never.

She didn't do anything she would regret. Not that night at least. Lucas was cute and he was interested in her and there was no one in the background, keeping tabs on her. For the first time ever she could do as she pleased. And she wanted to kiss Lucas.

'Have you made up your mind yet?' he asked.

He bent his head. His lips were millimetres from hers.

She'd wanted a chance to make a decision for herself. But some decisions, once made, couldn't be reversed. Right then, though, she wasn't to know that this kiss would mark the moment when she stood at the crossroads of her life. She wasn't to know that this would be the moment when she decided on a path that would change her life for ever.

She nodded, ever so slightly, and closed her eyes in a silent invitation.

His lips were soft. The pressure of his mouth on hers was gentle at first until his tongue darted between her lips, forcing her mouth open. She let him taste her as she explored him too. She felt as though he'd taken over her body. She felt as if they had become one already, joined at the lips. Her nipples hardened and a line of fire travelled from her chest to her groin, igniting her internally until she thought she might go up in flames. Her body was on fire as she pushed against him, begging him to go deeper, to taste more of her.

She could feel herself falling in love with each second.

He could kiss her as much as he liked for the rest of for ever if he kissed like that.

CHAPTER FIVE

'JESS? JESS!'

Jess turned around from the window as the sound of Kristie's voice dragged her back to the present. She needed to focus. Judging by Kristie's tone, it seemed she might have been calling her for a while. 'What?'

'Lily was talking to you.'

'What are we doing tonight, Mummy?' Lily asked, but Jess couldn't think. Her mind was still filled with thoughts of Lucas and it took her a moment to come back to the present. She was distracted but that wasn't Lily's fault and it wasn't a good enough reason to ignore her daughter.

Kristie rescued her. 'How would you like to do something special with me, Lily?' she offered.

'Like what?'

'It'll be a surprise. I know you love surprises. Go and pack a bag with your pyjamas and a toothbrush while I think of something.'

Kristie waited for Lily to leave the room. 'You should ring Lucas and see if he's free for dinner.'

'What? Why?' How was it possible that Kristie could read her mind?

'I know you haven't stopped thinking about him

since this morning, probably since yesterday. I know you said you were going to avoid him but you can't pretend you don't want to see him. You've been miles away all afternoon. So the way I figure it is you might as well go and see him while I'm here to look after Lily. I'll take her on a sleigh ride, she's desperate to do that—she won't even care what you're doing.'

'She told you she wants to go on a sleigh ride?' That was enough to stop Jess from thinking about Lucas. 'Would you mind doing something else? I really want to do that with her. I'm saving up to take her as a Christmas surprise.' Her heart ached. She knew Lily wanted to take a sleigh ride from Crystal Lodge more than anything and even now that she knew Lucas's involvement with the lodge she wasn't going to let it derail her plans. Logistics weren't the issue but money was. She didn't have the cash to spare so, until she got her first pay cheque, the sleigh ride would have to wait.

Jess could see Kristie biting her tongue and knew she wanted to offer to pay for it but she'd learnt the hard way that Jess was determined to make it on her own.

Kristie looked at her but didn't argue the point. 'Sure. Can I take her to our apartment?' she asked. 'I won't tell her it belongs to our family—we can drink hot chocolate and toast marshmallows in front of the fire and watch the replay of the Thanksgiving parade. She can have a sleepover and then you can have the night free to do as you please.'

Jess wasn't convinced this was a good idea. 'You know what happened last time we hatched a plan like that,' she said. 'I ended up pregnant.'

Kristie just shrugged and smiled. 'Lily would like a sibling. She'd probably like a father too. I think this is fate intervening. Leading you to decisions that I know you don't want to make. Perhaps you should let fate dictate to you. I think you owe it to Lucas to meet up. Don't you?'

'No,' Jess replied.

She'd refused to wear a dress. As if that meant she had some control over the situation. She didn't want to feel like she was going on a date. They were just two old acquaintances catching up. She tucked her jeans into her boots and tugged a black turtleneck sweater over her head. Jess did put on make-up—she was too vain not to—but kept it simple. Foundation, mascara, some blush and lip gloss. She still wanted to look pretty but not desperate. Adding a red scarf for some colour, she headed out the door.

She'd insisted on meeting him at the hotel. This wasn't a date so he didn't need to collect her, she was quite capable of walking a few streets. She stepped from the plaza into the lodge. Tonight she had more time to take in her surroundings and she stopped briefly, gathering her thoughts as she admired the room. There were two beautifully decorated Christmas trees in the lobby, one at each end, and the lobby itself was festooned with lights, pine branches, red bows and mistletoe.

The lodge was celebrating Christmas in style and decorations were multiplying in the village too. The Christmas spirit was alive and flourishing in Moose River and Jess smiled to herself. As a child she had loved Christmas. She had looked forward to it all year, partly because the festive season also included her birthday, but it had been her favourite time of year for so many reasons. Until her brother had died.

After Stephen's death Christmas had lost its sparkle. She knew he was always in her parents' thoughts, particularly her mother's, especially at certain times of the year, including Christmas, and that had taken the shine off the festivities. Even though he wasn't spoken of for fear of further upsetting her mother there was always the underlying sense that someone was missing and Christmas had never been the same. Until Lily was born. And now Jess was desperate to have the perfect Christmas. She wanted to create that for Lily and she had hoped that being in Moose River would give her that chance. This was her opportunity to put the sparkle back.

She felt someone watching her and she knew it was Lucas. Jess turned her head. He had been waiting for her by the bar and now he was walking towards her, coming to meet her in the lobby.

Seeing him coming for her made her feel as if she was coming home but she resisted the feeling. She belonged here in Moose River so she should already feel at home, she shouldn't need Lucas to make her feel that way.

He was wearing a navy suit with a crisp white shirt and a tie the colour of forget-me-nots. She'd never seen him in a suit before. His hair had been brushed, it wasn't as tousled as she was used to, and she fought the urge to run her fingers through it and mess it up a bit. He looked handsome but she preferred him more casually styled. But perhaps the old Lucas wouldn't have fitted into this fancy hotel. She wondered how much he'd changed. Probably not as much as she had. The thought made her smile again.

He smiled in response. A dimple appeared in his

cheek, a sparkle in his eye. Now he looked like the Lucas she'd fallen in love with.

He reached out and took both her hands in his then leaned down and kissed her cheek, enveloping her in his clean, fresh scent. The caress of his lips sent tingles through her as her body responded to his touch. She could feel every beat of her heart and every whisper of air that brushed past her face as his lips left their imprint on her skin. Despite what she thought, her body didn't seem to remember that this wasn't a date or that seven years had passed. Her body reacted as if it had been yesterday that Lucas had been in her bed.

She'd been on a few dates over the past few years but she'd eventually given up because no one else had ever had the same effect on her as Lucas had. The attraction she'd felt for Lucas had been immediate, powerful and irresistible, and she'd never felt the same connection with anyone else. Not one other man had ever made her feel like she might melt with desire. Not one of them had made her feel like she was the centre of the universe, a universe that might explode at any moment. What was the point in dating? she'd asked herself. Why waste time and energy on someone who wasn't Lucas? If she couldn't have Lucas she'd rather have nothing.

And it seemed he hadn't lost the ability to make her feel truly alive. Just a touch, a glance, a kiss could set her off. She'd need to be careful. She'd need to keep her wits about her and remember what was at stake.

'JJ,' he said, and his voice washed over her, soft and deep and intimate. How could she feel so much when so little was said? 'Thank you for coming.'

As if she'd had a choice.

Despite her show of determination to Kristie earlier

in the day, she'd known her resolve wasn't strong enough to withstand the temptation of knowing that Lucas was only a few streets away. She'd known she'd pick up the phone and call him.

'I hope you don't mind if we stay in the hotel to eat?' he asked.

'I'm not dressed to eat here,' she said, as she took her hands out of his hold and shrugged out of her coat. Jeans and an old sweater were not five-star dining attire, even if the jeans hugged her curves and the black top made her blonde hair shine like white gold.

He ran his eyes over her and Jess could feel her temperature rise by a degree for every second she spent under his gaze. She could see the appreciation in his eyes and the attention felt good.

'You look lovely,' he said as he took her coat. It had been a long time since she'd wanted to capture a man's interest and despite telling herself this wasn't a date it was nice to know that Lucas liked what he could see. 'And you're safe with me. I can put in a good word for you if need be.' He was laughing at her and she relaxed. His words reminded her of their first night together all those years ago. She'd felt safe then and she felt safe now.

'Are you sure? I don't want to drag down the standards.'

'Believe me, you're not lowering our standards.' He ran his gaze over her again and Jess's breath caught in her throat as she saw his forget-me-not-blue eyes darken. 'We're fully booked for the weekend and I'd like to be close to hand in case there are any issues.'

She was worried that eating in the hotel would give him the upper hand. He would be in familiar surroundings and she felt underdressed and out of place. But, then again, she consoled herself, this wasn't a competition, it was a friendly dinner.

'Are you expecting problems?' she asked, as she walked beside him into the restaurant. He had his hand resting lightly in the small of her back, guiding her forward. His touch was so light she should hardly have felt it but she could swear she could feel each individual fingertip and her skin was on fire under the thin wool of her sweater.

'There are always teething problems with a new project—the only unknown is the scale of the disaster,' he said, as he checked in her coat and greeted the maître d'.

She followed him to a table positioned beside the large picture windows looking out over the outdoor terrace and onto the plaza. Lucas pulled out her chair for her and reached for a bottle of champagne that was chilling in a bucket next to her. He popped the cork and poured them each a glass.

'To old friends,' she said, as they touched glasses.

'And new memories,' he added. 'It's good to see you, JJ.'

She took a nervous sip of her champagne as the waiter approached their table.

'We're not ready to order yet,' Lucas told him.

'It's fine, Lucas,' Jess told him. 'You must know what's good—why don't you choose for us both?' She sounded breathless. She was nervous, on edge from conflicting emotions—guilt, lust, fear and desire—and she doubted she'd be able to eat anything anyway. The sooner he ordered the sooner she'd be able to escape before she said or did something she might regret. She'd been desperate to see him but now she was worried that she'd made a mistake.

She looked out the window as Lucas gave the waiter their order. Christmas lights were strung up around the terrace and stretched across to the plaza. They surrounded the ice-skating rink and looped through the bare branches of the trees. The ice and snow sparkled under the glow of the lights as skaters glided around the rink. It was the perfect image of a winter wonderland.

'It's a beautiful view,' she said, as the waiter departed, leaving them alone again. She got her breathing under control and returned her gaze to Lucas. 'It's a beautiful hotel.'

'You like it?'

'It's perfect. Just looking at it makes me happy. Someone has done a very good job.' The entire lodge—the furnishings in the rooms, the decorations in the lobby and the views from the restaurant—all conspired to make her feel as though the hotel was giving her a warm hug. Or maybe that was Lucas.

'Thank you,' he said.

'You?'

Lucas nodded. 'This is my vision.'

'Really? I thought you were the hotel manager.'

'That's my official title but this is my hotel.'

'Yours? You own it?'

'Yes. This is my baby.'

'You dream big, don't you?' she said.

'What do you mean?'

'You told me you wanted to work in the hospitality industry when you finished university. You never said you actually wanted to own a hotel.'

'You remember that?'

I remember everything about you, she thought, but she said nothing. She just nodded as the waiter placed their first course on their table.

'I have you to thank for that,' he told her.

'Me?'

'I started planning this the day you vanished from my life.'

'I didn't vanish,' she objected. 'My father dragged me away. I didn't have a choice.'

'In my mind you vanished. I never saw you again. I looked for you, every day, until the end of the season, until the day I left, but you had disappeared.'

'You looked for me?' She'd never dared to imagine that he would have thought about her.

'Of course. Did you think I would just let you go? Especially after what happened that day. I went back to your apartment the next day but there was no answer. Eventually I found the caretaker and he told me you'd all left. I was sure you would get in touch with me and I kept looking, thinking maybe you'd be back before the season ended. When that didn't happen I started writing to you, long letters that I was going to post to your family's apartment, but I never finished them.'

'Why not?' How much simpler might things have been if he'd done that. Then she might have been able to find him when she'd needed to.

'I was never good with words. I decided that words were empty promises and that I was better off showing you what I wanted you to know. It's taken longer than I thought. But now we have a chance to fill in all the gaps. To catch up on what happened that day and in the past seven years.'

Jess could remember every second of that day. Every

moment was imprinted on her brain, each glorious moment, along with every humiliating one. It had certainly been a birthday to remember.

She had wanted to sleep with him from the moment he'd kissed her. After that first night at his party she would have gladly given him anything he'd asked for but for as long as she could remember she'd fantasised about her first sexual experience and it had involved a big bed, clean sheets, flowers, music and candles. Not a single bed in a shared flat. Getting naked in Lucas's flat in a bedroom he'd shared with Sam had not been an option and so she'd had to wait and hope for a different opportunity. And then, on the morning of her birthday, her aunt and uncle had announced they were going cat skiing, leaving the girls on their own, leaving Jess free to spend the afternoon with Lucas.

They had spent any spare moments they'd had together since meeting seven days earlier. With Kristie's help Jess had sneaked off at every chance she'd had. She'd never done anything like that before but being with Lucas was more important than being the perfect daughter. Lucas had unleashed another side to her personality and she hadn't been able to resist him.

On her eighteenth birthday her aunt and uncle's plans had given her the ideal opportunity to create the perfect setting in which to let Lucas seduce her. It had to be that way. Lucas would have to seduce her as she didn't know where to start. She would create the opportunity for seduction and Lucas would have to do the rest.

And, just as Kristie had predicted several days earlier, Jess found herself planning sneaky afternoon sex. Only it had been more than that. She had gifted her virginity to Lucas. She had offered herself to him. She had offered him her body and her heart and he had taken them both. She had given herself to Lucas and in return he had given her Lily. It had been the perfect birthday. Up to a point.

'That day didn't end quite how I'd expected,' she said.

'No. Me neither. But I have to know what happened to you. Where did you go?'

'We left Moose River that night.'

'All of you?'

Jess nodded.

'Because of me?' Lucas asked.

'Because of both of us,' Jess said. 'But mostly because of my father. I still don't know how I'd forgotten they were arriving that night. I can't believe I lost track of time so badly.' She'd been swept away by Lucas and once she'd had a taste of him she hadn't been able to get enough. He had brought her to life. Her body had blossomed under the touch of his fingers and the caress of his lips. He had introduced her to a whole new world. A world of pleasure, fulfilment and ecstasy. He had consumed her body, her mind and her heart, and she had forgotten about everything else, including the imminent arrival of her parents.

Everyone had got more than they'd bargained for that day.

Jess could still remember the moment she'd heard them arrive. The moment her ecstasy had turned to dread. The moment her fantasy had become a nightmare.

Lucas's head had been buried between her thighs and he had just given her another orgasm, her second of the day, when she'd heard the front door of the apartment slam. And then she'd heard Kristie's loud, panicked voice welcoming them. Jess had known Kristie had been trying to warn her. Thank God she'd been there and had been able to stall them just long enough for Lucas to scramble to the bathroom. Jess could still recall how his round white buttocks, pale in contrast to his Aussie tan, had flexed as he'd darted to the bathroom. She'd just had time to throw his clothes in after him and then pull on her sweatpants and a T-shirt before her father had come into her room to wish her a happy birthday.

Their hurried dressing hadn't been enough to fool him. He'd taken one look at their semi-dressed state and the rumpled bed and had gone completely berserk. Being caught out by her parents hadn't been anywhere near how she'd imagined that afternoon would end.

Her father had been furious with her, upset and disappointed, and disparaging of Lucas. He'd thrown him out without ceremony after a few well-chosen remarks before making Jess pack her bags. Her aunt and uncle had arrived home from their day of cat skiing in the middle of the circus and both girls had then been bundled into the car and returned to Vancouver, where Jess had been subjected to endless lectures about abuse of trust and lack of respect for her aunt and uncle as well as for her parents' rules.

'I was so worried about you.' Lucas's words broke into her reverie. 'I thought your father was going to have a fit.'

'He was always over-protective but his reaction was extreme, even by his standards. I was so embarrassed by the way he spoke to you. I still haven't forgiven him for that.'

Lucas smiled as the waiter delivered their appetisers. 'I feel I should thank him.'

'*Thank* him?'

Lucas nodded. 'His diatribe started me on this mission. He accused me of being a good-for-nothing bum and I wanted to prove him wrong.'

Jess looked around her at the opulent hotel. 'You did all this to get back at my father?'

'I wanted to prove to him that I was worthy of his daughter. He was my inspiration but I did this for you.'

'For me?'

He picked up her hand and Jess felt his pulse shoot through her. His thumb traced lazy circles in her palm and her body lit up in response to his touch. It gave life to her cells and awakened her dormant senses. She felt seventeen again, full of newly awakened hormones.

'Your father suggested I would never measure up to his expectations. But it was your expectations I was worried about. I wanted to be someone who was important to you. I wanted to be someone who could fight for you. Who could protect you. I didn't stand up for you that night and I want you to know that won't happen again.'

'I'm not the same person I was then, Lucas.'

She remembered that awful day as if it were yesterday. The shame. The heartbreak. She had felt as though things could never be worse. Until she'd found out that, really, they could. In fact, they could be a *lot* worse.

Everything had changed after that, including her. The only thing that hadn't changed, apparently, over the past seven years was how Lucas affected her. As his eyes locked onto hers she knew she would jump right back into bed with him tonight if he asked. She could feel every cell in her body yearning for him. She felt as though if she didn't keep tight control of her emotions her body would dissolve. The heat between them was enough to melt her core and she could feel herself burning.

She could get lost in him so easily and she couldn't let that happen. She needed to resist him, needed to keep her distance, but when he looked at her like he was doing now, like she was the only person in the world, she didn't think she had the willpower to stay away. Sitting there, looking in to his blue eyes, she could pretend that her life was still simple and easy and privileged.

But that wasn't the truth.

She fought the urge to give in to him. To do so would mean telling him all her secrets. She knew that it was inevitable but she was terrified of what he would think when he found out. Would he forgive her? Would he reject her? Would he reject them both?

What a complicated situation. Coming back was supposed to be the answer. It was supposed to help her get her life on track, to give her and Lily the freedom she craved, but all she'd got were complications and confusion. All she'd got were more questions and fewer answers.

She suspected it would be impossible to get out of this with her heart intact and she wasn't sure if she could stand to lose him a second time. But that wasn't going to be her choice to make.

She picked up her glass as it gave her a chance to remove her hand from his, which was the only thing to do if she wanted to think straight. There were things she needed to tell him.

Jess sipped her champagne, steadying the glass on her lip to disguise the shake in her hand. All the times she'd wished he'd been with her and now here he was.

It was time for the truth. She couldn't keep her secret any longer. She took a deep breath and put her glass down on the table. Starting the tale would be difficult but she feared it wouldn't be the worst part.

'Lucas, there's something I need to tell you.'

CHAPTER SIX

'I'M SORRY TO INTERRUPT, Mr White, but there's an emergency.'

Before Jess could begin to explain, before she could begin to divulge the secrets she'd been keeping, she was interrupted by a tall, thin, young woman dressed impeccably in a tailored black skirt suit, who appeared beside their table. The gold name tag on her lapel read 'Sofia' and her dark hair, cut in a shiny blunt bob, brushed her shoulders as she leant over to speak to Lucas.

'What is it?'

'A child is missing.'

Lucas was out of his seat before Sofia had finished her sentence. 'Are they hotel guests?' he asked.

'No.' Sofia named one of the smaller lodges and Jess recognised the name. It was an old lodge on the edge of the village. 'The search and rescue team has been mobilised but because of the heavy snowfalls they are having trouble finding tracks and have requested all hands on deck.'

'Of course.' Lucas turned to Jess. 'I'm sorry, I'll have to go. I'm part of the volunteer S&R team. We assist the professionals when we're needed.'

'Is there anything I can do?' Jess asked.

'What did you have in mind?'

'I don't know. I could help to look or at least make cups of tea. Someone always does that job.' There had to be something she could do.

'Sofia, can you see if you can rustle up some warmer clothes for Jess and some snow boots while I get changed?'

Jess took that to mean he had given permission for her to accompany him and she followed Sofia and got changed as quickly as possible. She didn't want to hold Lucas up.

Outside the snow was still falling. The Christmas lights around the plaza were doing their best to shine through the weather as Jess wondered what sort of Christmas the family of the little boy would get. She hoped he'd be found.

She could see pinpricks of light throughout the village and up and down the mountain. The lights bobbed in the darkness as the searchers panned their flashlights across the snow. There had to be hundreds of them.

The snow muffled all sound but Jess could hear the occasional voice calling out a name. Otherwise, the village was eerily quiet and Jess guessed that the S&R team didn't want any unnecessary noise that might mask something important. Like the cry of a young child.

Lucas strode out, heading for the lodge where the little boy had gone missing and where the S&R was now being co-ordinated. Jess hurried along beside him. When she slipped on the snow he reached for her hand to steady her. He kept hold of her as they approached the lodge from the rear but he wasn't talking. Jess assumed he was focusing on what lay ahead and she kept quiet too. She didn't want to disturb him or any of the other people who were out searching.

They reached the lodge and Lucas held the door open for her and followed her inside. He made his way directly to a table that had been set up in a lounge area to the right of the entrance and introduced himself to the man who was sitting there. He had a two-way radio in one hand and a large map spread out in front of him.

'The boy's name is Michael. He is seven years old and he was reported missing twenty minutes ago.' The search co-ordinator gave them the little information he had.

'Where was he last seen?'

'He and his brothers were playing in the snow behind the lodge. His brothers came inside thinking he was behind them but he wasn't.'

'Where is the search area?' Lucas peppered the man with questions.

'The lodge is at the epicentre of the search and we've spread out from here. There are people searching at one-hundred-metre intervals from here.' The co-ordinator pointed to concentric circles that had been marked on the map with red pen. 'This is the area we're covering so far.'

'Can someone show me exactly where he was last seen?'

'If you go around the back of the lodge you'll see the snowman the boys were making. That was the last confirmed sighting.'

'I'd like to start from there,' Lucas said, 'unless there's anywhere more specific you want me to begin?'

'There was no sign of him there.'

'I'd like to check again.' Something about Lucas's tone suggested he wasn't really asking for permission. He was a man with a plan.

The co-ordinator nodded. 'Okay. Take these with you,' he said, as he handed him a whistle and a torch.

Lucas turned to Jess. 'JJ, come with me.'

Jess followed him back outside with no real idea about what he expected of her or how much help she could be. She'd have to trust him to direct her.

She hurried to keep up with him as he stomped through the snow around to the back of the lodge. Jess's borrowed boots sank into the snowdrifts that had formed against the walls of the lodge and she was out of breath by the time she rounded the back corner. A lonely, misshapen snowman stared at her as she gulped in the cold air.

Lucas was standing beside the snowman, looking left and right. The snow around the snowman had been flattened and trampled by dozens of feet, the searchers' feet, Jess assumed, although most traces were already being covered by the fresh snow that continued to fall. Jess knew the footsteps of Michael and his brothers would have been obliterated long ago, making the search even more difficult.

Lucas lifted his head and Jess could see him looking up at the roof of the lodge.

'What are you looking for?' she asked.

He took three steps towards the lodge and stopped beside a large mound of fresh snow, which looked as though it had been pushed into a heavy drift by a snowplough. 'This pile of snow has fallen from the roof.' He pointed up to the roof. 'See how that section of roof is clear of snow?' Above their heads a large section of the lodge roof was bare. The weight of the fresh snowfall had caused the snow beneath to slide off the roof and land in a heap on the ground, a heap that was five or six feet high. 'I've seen this once before. We need to check this drift. Michael could be buried under here.'

Lucas knelt in the snow and started digging with his gloved hands while Jess stared at the huge mound. She felt her chest tighten with anxiety and she struggled to breathe. She felt as though she was the one trapped and suffocating.

How long had Michael been missing? It must be close to half an hour by now. *How long can someone survive without air?* Not long.

She knew that. She'd lived that. Her own brother had suffocated.

Jess was frozen to the spot, paralysed by the memories. She couldn't go through this again.

'JJ, give me a hand.' Lucas was looking at her over his shoulder. His busyness was in stark contrast to her immobility but she didn't think she could move.

'JJ, get down here.'

Lucas raised his voice and his words bounced off the walls of the lodge and echoed across the snow, jolting Jess out of her motionless state.

She knelt down beside him and started digging. If she didn't want to go through this again she only had one option and that was to do everything in her power to save this child. Digging like a mad woman now, she could feel the sweat running between her breasts and her arms ached with the effort of shifting the snow, but she wasn't going to let this be another tragedy. She hadn't been able to save her brother but she'd been eight years old then. She wasn't going to let another little boy die.

'Michael, are you there, buddy? Hang on, we're

going to get you out.' Lucas was talking constantly as he frantically tore at the snow.

Jess's vision was blurring as the blood pumped through her muscles. Her breaths were coming in short bursts and her heart was pounding but she wasn't about to stop. She dug her hands into the pile of snow again and her fingers hit something hard. Something firmer than the recently fallen snow.

'Lucas! There's something here.'

Lucas helped her to scrape the snow away and Jess could see something dark in the snow pile. Clothing? A jacket?

'It's a boot,' he said. 'Keep clearing the snow,' he told her as he pulled the whistle from his pocket and blew into it hard. The shrill sound pierced the still night air and Jess knew it would be heard for miles. Lucas gave three, short, sharp blasts on the whistle before yelling, 'Some help over here.'

Jess's movements intensified. She had to hurry. She had to clear this snow.

'What is it?'

'Have you found him?'

They were bombarded with questions as other searchers arrived on the scene.

'He's here,' Lucas replied. 'We need to clear this snow.'

Jess had cleared the snow to expose Michael's foot and ankle and now that they could work out in which direction he was lying Lucas could direct others to start clearing the snow to expose Michael's head. There was a sense of urgency, though the snow muffled the sound so there was nothing loud about the panic but it was there, under the surface. Every minute was vital, every second precious.

In under a minute the snow had been cleared to reveal a child's body. A young boy, curled into a foetal position with one arm thrown up to cover his face. He wasn't moving.

'Call the ambos,' Lucas said to the crowd that had gathered around them. He whipped off one of his gloves and placed his fingers on the boy's neck to feel for a pulse. 'Pulse is slow but present.'

Jess bent her head and put her cheek against Michael's nose. 'He's not breathing.'

'We need to roll him,' Lucas said. 'Clear some snow from behind him.'

'I can't let this happen again, Lucas. We have to save him.'

'We're doing everything we can, JJ.'

'We have to hurry.'

The snow had been cleared now and Jess held the boy's head gently between her palms as Lucas rolled him. Stuffing her gloves into her pocket, she started mouth-to-mouth resuscitation as they waited for the ambulance. She had to do something. She had to try to save his life.

Clearing Michael's airway, she tipped his head back slightly and breathed into his mouth, watching for the rise and fall of his chest. She was aware of his parents arriving on the scene as she continued to breathe air into their son's lungs. She heard them but she couldn't stop to look up. Everything else had to be blocked out. She could feel tears on her cheeks but she couldn't stop to wipe them away, she had to keep going.

'JJ, the ambos are here.' Lucas rested his hand on her shoulder and finally she could stop and hand over to someone who was better qualified than her.

She was shaking as Lucas helped her to her feet. She knew the tip of her nose was red and cold and she could feel the tightness of the skin on her cheeks where the tears had dried and left salt stains. Her toes were numb and her fingers were freezing.

Lucas put his arm around her. 'Come on, let's get you warmed up.'

She knew Lucas wanted to get her out of the cold and she knew she should probably listen to him but she couldn't do it. 'I can't leave yet,' she told him, as she pulled her gloves back onto her hands. She had to stay. She had to know how this ended.

Lucas didn't argue. He kept his arm around her as they stood together while the ambulance officers inserted an artificial airway and attached an ambu bag and Jess was grateful for his additional warmth. She could hear that the ambos were worried about head and thoracic injuries but they weren't giving much away. They ran a drip of warm saline and loaded Michael onto a stretcher as they continued to bag him. At least they hadn't given up.

Jess and Lucas waited until the ambulance drove away, heading for the hospital, and then, somehow, Lucas wangled a lift for them back to Crystal Lodge.

Jess was exhausted and Lucas practically carried her inside when they reached the lodge. 'Do you want me to run you home?' he asked.

'Not yet.' She could barely keep her eyes open but she wanted to stay in Lucas's embrace for just a little longer.

'Come to my suite, then, and I'll organise something warm to drink.'

Jess didn't have the energy to argue, even if she'd wanted to. He led her into an office behind the reception desk and unlocked a door in the back wall. The door opened into the living room of his suite. The room was cosy and, even better, it was warm.

Lucas steered her towards the leather couch that was positioned in front of a fireplace. A wood fire burned in the grate. It was probably only for decoration—Jess assumed there would be central heating—but there was something comforting about a proper wood fire.

He undid her boots and pulled them from her feet. He rubbed the soles of her feet, encouraging the blood back into her extremities, and Jess almost groaned aloud with pleasure.

There was a knock on the door as Lucas propped her feet on the ottoman and one of the housekeeping staff wheeled in a small trolley. 'Dessert, Mr White.'

Lucas lifted the lid to reveal a chocolate pudding, apple pie and a mug of eggnog.

He took the eggnog and added some brandy and rum to it from bottles that stood on a small sideboard. 'That'll warm you up,' he said, as he passed it to Jess before pouring himself a shot of rum. He dropped a soft blanket over Jess's lap and sat down beside her. She lay next to him with her feet stretched out to the fire and his arm wrapped around her shoulders. Lying in front of the fire in Lucas's embrace with a warm drink and warm apple pie, she thought this might be heaven.

'Do you think Michael will be all right?' she asked.

'He has a good chance. His pulse was slow but the cold temperature means his systems had shut down and that may save him.'

'But we have no idea how long he wasn't breathing.'

'Maybe he'd only just stopped breathing. If there was an air pocket in front of his face he could have survived for thirty minutes or maybe a little longer in those conditions, provided the snow wasn't heavy enough to crush him. We'll just have to hope that we found him in time.'

'How did you know where to look for him?'

'I saw a similar scenario once before in Australia when a child was in the wrong place at the wrong time and was buried by a pile of snow that slid off a roof. No one picked up on it at the time so people were searching in the wrong places. It's stuck with me. I'll never forget the possibility that that can happen.'

'What happened that time?'

Lucas shook his head. 'We weren't so fortunate back then. By the time we found him it was too late. We were lucky tonight.' He took a sip of his rum. 'You said you couldn't let this happen again. You know what it's like, don't you? To lose someone. You've been in that situation before too, haven't you?'

Jess nodded.

'Do you want to talk about it?'

'It was my brother.'

'Your brother?' She could hear the frown in his voice and his arm around her shoulders squeezed her against him a little more firmly.

She let her head drop onto his shoulder. 'He died when he was six.'

'In an accident?'

'Yes, one that had a lot of similarities to tonight.'

'Was it here?'

'No. We spent most of our winter holidays here but Mum used to take my brother and me to spend our summer holidays in California with her family. Dad would join us for a week or two but it was usually just Mum and her sisters and our cousins and we'd spend the summer at my grandparents' beach house. We loved it. We were pretty much allowed to do as we pleased for six weeks. That summer we were digging a big hole with tunnels under the sand. We'd done this before but not with tunnels and one of the tunnels collapsed, trapping Stephen and one of my cousins in it. We managed to get my cousin out but not Stephen. The weight of the sand crushed him and he suffocated. His body was recovered but it was too late.'

'JJ, that's awful. I'm so sorry.' Lucas dropped a kiss on her forehead, just above her temple. It felt like a reflex response but it lifted her spirits. 'How old were you when it happened?'

'Eight.' Jess sipped her eggnog. She could feel the warmth flow through her and the kick of the added brandy gave her the courage to continue. 'My mother has never gotten over it. I think she feels a lot of guilt for not watching us more closely but we'd done similar things plenty of times before without any disasters. I think the combination of stress and guilt and trauma was all too much. We've never been back to California. Stephen's death cast a shadow over our family, a shadow I've grown up under, and it's shaped my life. I didn't want another family to go through what we've been through.'

'What did it do to you?'

'After he died my mother changed. She couldn't be around people. She couldn't bear the thought that they would ask about Stephen or ask how she was coping. She wasn't coping. With anything. She shut herself off from everyone, including me. Dad said she couldn't cope with the idea that something might happen to me too so her way of coping was to ignore the outside world and me.

'Dad, however, was determined that nothing was going to happen to me. One tragedy was enough. So I was protected, very closely and very deliberately. I wasn't allowed any freedom. Mum and Dad had to know where I was and what I was doing every minute of the day, which is why Dad flipped out when he caught us together. His whole mission in life had become to protect me from harm and there I was, in bed with a stranger. His reaction was completely out of proportion with what we'd been doing but it was a case of his mind jumping to the worst possible conclusions of not knowing what else I'd been up to without his knowledge. My whole life has been influenced by Stephen's death. In a way it's still influencing me.'

'How?'

'It had a lot to do with why I came back here with Lily.'

'Lily? That's your daughter?'

Jess nodded. She hadn't realised she hadn't told him her name. She wondered if he liked it.

'Before Stephen died I was allowed to walk to school with my friends and go on sleepovers and school camps. After he died that all changed. I didn't want Lily to grow up like that. But because I'd spent most of my childhood being taught to be fearful I found it hard to relax. When she was a baby I was very uptight, I was worried about what she ate and panicked every time she got a cold.

'I was nervous about leaving her with childminders while I studied and worked and when she started school I realised that I was bringing her up the same way my parents had brought me up. I was wrapping her in cotton wool and I didn't want that. I wanted her to have the childhood that I'd missed out on. I wanted her to be able to walk to school and to her friends' houses without me worrying that something would happen to her. I wanted her to grow up somewhere safe.'

'And what about Lily's father? What does he think about you moving here?'

'Lily doesn't know her father.'

'Really? What happened to him?'

Was now the right time to tell him? No, she decided, she needed to have a fresh mind.

'Sorry,' he apologised, when she didn't answer straight away. 'It's probably none of my business.'

If only he knew how much of his business it actually was.

She had to tell him something. 'Nothing happened to him. I was young. We both were.' She tipped her head up and looked at Lucas, met his forget-me-not-blue eyes and willed him to understand what she was saying. 'I loved him very much but our timing was wrong. It was no one's fault but Lily and I have been on our own for as long as she can remember.'

She knew she had to tell him about Lily but where did she start? *How* should she start?

She stifled a yawn. It was too late to have this conversation tonight; they were both exhausted. A little voice in her head was telling her that she was making excuses but she didn't have the emotional energy to have the discussion now.

She pushed herself into a sitting position. 'It's getting late,' she said, making yet another excuse. 'I'd better get home.'

'Are you sure? I hate to think of you going out in the cold just when you've thawed out.' She could hear the smile in his voice and knew she couldn't afford to look at him. If she saw him smiling at her she'd find it hard to refuse. Although he might not be intending to cause trouble he'd done it once before and she suspected it could easily happen again.

Mischief and mayhem. That's how she'd first thought of him and it still seemed to fit. Mischief, mayhem and trouble.

She was tempted to stay right where she was, on the couch in front of the fire wrapped in Lucas's arms. It felt safe. Lily was having a sleepover with Kristie so she could do it but she knew that it would just complicate the situation. Seven years ago she'd fallen for the charms of a good-looking boy and she knew she could easily fall again. She couldn't let herself get involved.

She reached for her boots, busying herself with putting them back on. 'I have to go. I have Lily, remember?'

'I'll walk you home, then.' Lucas stood and took her hand to pull her to her feet. He helped her into her coat and then took her hand again as they walked through the village. She kept her hand in his. There was no harm in that, right?

'This is where you're living?' He sounded surprised to find she was in the old accommodation block. 'We're back where it all began.'

He pushed open the door and Jess knocked the snow from her boots before stepping into the foyer. She hesitated inside, not wanting Lucas to walk her to her door, afraid of too much temptation.

'Thanks for getting me home safely and thank you for an interesting evening.' She sounded so formal but that was good. She was keeping her distance.

'My pleasure. We should do it again.' Lucas's voice was far from formal. It was full of promise and suggestion and Jess could feel her body respond. If he could do that to her with his voice she hated to think what he could do with a touch.

'Without the drama,' she said, as she fought for control. She was still conflicted and confused. She could feel the attraction but she knew she couldn't pursue it. Not yet. She couldn't let her hormones dictate to her.

'Definitely.' Lucas's voice was a whisper. He bent his head and his lips were beside her ear. Then beside her mouth.

Her hormones took over again as confusion gave way to desire. She wasn't strong enough to resist him. She never had been.

She turned her head and then his lips were covering hers. He wrapped his arms around her waist and pulled her close. Her hands went behind his head and kept him there. She parted her lips and tasted him. He tasted of rum and chocolate. He tasted like a grown-up version of the Lucas she'd fallen in love with.

His kiss was still so familiar and it made her heart ache with longing. She had seven years of hopes and dreams stored inside her and Lucas's lips were the key that released them. They flooded through her and her body sang as it remembered him. Remembered how he tasted and felt.

His body was still firm and hard. His hair was thick. He smelt like winter and tasted like summer. He felt like home.

She clung to him, even though she knew she shouldn't be kissing him. She knew she was only complicating matters further but she had no resistance when it came to Lucas. Absolutely none. She knew she'd have to find some.

She pulled back.

'We should definitely do *that* again,' he said as he grinned at her, and she was tempted to take him up on his suggestion there and then.

No. Find some resistance. Find some resolve, she told herself, and find it right now. 'I'm not sure that's wise.'

'Don't blame me.' He pointed up and she saw a sprig of mistletoe hanging from the ceiling. 'Someone has gone to all that effort, I thought it would be a shame to let it go to waste.'

A shame indeed. She smiled but she'd have to let it go for now. She wanted the fantasy but she was worried that the reality might be very different.

CHAPTER SEVEN

'LUCAS, WE HAVE a situation.'

Lucas looked up from his computer screen. His PA was standing in his doorway, smiling. She didn't look too perturbed by the 'situation'.

'What is it?'

'I think you'd better come and see,' Sofia replied.

Lucas followed her out of his office. He glanced around as he crossed the lobby. Everything looked to be in order. Sofia continued across the floor and exited the lodge out onto the plaza. It was late in the afternoon, the ski runs had closed and streams of people were coming and going through the village. Sofia gestured with an open palm towards the bay where the lodge sleigh was parked. Three young girls, one with her platinum blonde hair tied in two short pigtails, stood beside it.

Lily. Even if he hadn't seen her at the tube park last weekend he would have recognised her. She was just a down-sized version of her mother.

Lucas frowned. What possible reason could Lily have for being here? It had been almost a week since he'd seen Jess and he'd never met her daughter.

Since the kiss, he'd been snowed under with work, the hotel was at full capacity and he'd had some staffing and maintenance issues that had taken up a lot of his time, and although he had invited Jess and Lily to dinner during the week Jess had graciously refused. He wasn't sure if she was avoiding him or not but he'd been too busy to push the invitation. Nevertheless, his curiosity was now piqued.

'What do they want?' he asked Sofia.

'A sleigh ride.'

'I've got this,' he told her.

He'd been kicking himself since last weekend when he'd discovered that Jess had a child. He couldn't believe he'd been such an idiot. He should have come back to Moose River sooner. He'd thought he'd had time, he'd thought he could afford to wait until he'd achieved his goals. They were both young and he hadn't considered for one moment that Jess would have moved on. Not to this extent.

But a child wasn't a deal-breaker. Not in any way. If Jess had been married, that would be a different ball game but he could work with her being a mother. If she'd let him. And he was intrigued to find out more about Lily. This might be the perfect opportunity.

He approached the girls. One looked to be Lily's age, maybe a year older, and the other he guessed to be twelve or thirteen.

'Lily?' he asked. 'I'm Lucas. This is my hotel. Is there something I can do for you?'

Lily looked up at him and he was struck again by the resemblance to Jess. She was frowning and she got the same little crease between her eyebrows that her mother got when she was unsure of something. 'How did you know my name?' she asked.

Lucas smiled to himself. He'd been imagining that

Jess had mentioned him to Lily. He'd been flattered and encouraged to think she might have but obviously that wasn't the case.

'I know your mum. You look just like her. What can I do for you?'

'Is this your sleigh?' Lily asked, as she pointed at the brightly painted red sleigh that had 'Crystal Lodge' stencilled across the back of it in ornate gold lettering.

Lucas nodded. 'It is.'

'We wanted a sleigh ride. We have money but this man…' Lily looked up at François, the sleigh driver with an accusatory expression '…says he can't take us.'

'François isn't allowed to take you unless you have an adult with you,' Lucas explained.

Lily folded her arms across her chest and frowned. Lucas expected her to stamp her tiny feet next and he almost laughed before realising that would probably not be appreciated. Not if she was anything like her mother. Lily looked up at him with big green eyes that were nearly too big for her face. She was a *lot* like her mother. 'You could come with us,' she said.

'Me?'

Lily nodded. 'You said you know my mum. You could take us. We have money.'

'Where did you get the money from?'

'Annabel's mum,' Lily said.

Lucas turned to the other two girls. 'Is one of you Annabel?' he asked.

The older girl pointed to the younger one. 'She is,' she said. 'I'm Claire, her sister.'

'Is the money supposed to be for a sleigh ride?' Lucas asked.

Claire shook her head. 'No. We were going ice skating but Lily and Annabel ran off here.'

'Where is your mum?'

'She's at work,' Claire told him. 'She owns the bakery.'

'The patisserie?' he asked.

Lily giggled and her laughter set her pigtails swinging. 'You don't say it right,' she told him.

'Don't I? That's probably because I'm Australian. I don't speak French.'

'That's why you sound funny,' she said, as if everything made perfect sense now. 'I know all about Australia.'

'How much can you know? You're only five.'

'I am not. I'm six.'

Lucas was curious. He was sure Jess had told him Lily was five. 'How do you know about Australia?'

'My mum told me.'

Now he was even more curious. He'd been wondering about Jess's circumstances, he'd spent too much time in the past week thinking about her if he was honest, but there was a lot to consider. Why wasn't she living in her family's apartment? Why had she taken basic accommodation? And what had happened to Lily's father? Why wasn't he in the picture? And why would she talk to Lily about Australia? He couldn't ask Lily directly but he had another solution.

'I need to call your mum,' he told Claire. 'Would you girls like to meet Banjo while I do that?' he asked.

'Who's Banjo?'

'He's the horse.'

Lily and Annabel jumped up and down and clapped their hands.

'You've met François,' Lucas introduced the sleigh driver, 'and this is Banjo.' He was a handsome draught horse. He was dark brown but had distinctive white lower legs with heavy feathering and white markings on his face. Lucas rubbed his neck and the big horse nuzzled into his shoulder. 'Would you like to feed him? He loves apples.'

'Yes, please.' The girls all answered as one.

'Hold your hand flat like this,' Lucas took Lily's hand and flattened her fingers out. François passed him an apple that had been cut in half and he placed it in the centre of her palm. 'Banjo will take it off your hand but keep your hand flat.' He guided Lily's hand to the horse and held her fingers out of the way. 'He won't be able to see the apple so he'll sniff for it.'

Lily giggled as the horse's warm breath tickled her hand. He took the apple and Lucas let Lily rub his neck as he crunched it. Banjo shook his head and Lily pulled her hand away.

'François will give you each an apple to feed Banjo while I ring the patisserie,' Lucas said, as he took his cell phone from his pocket. He got the number and spoke to Fleur. He explained the situation and also explained he was an old friend of Jess's and offered to drop the girls off to her.

As he finished the call Sofia reappeared, carrying a small cardboard cake box, a flask and some takeaway coffee cups. 'What are those for?' Lucas asked.

'I thought the girls might like some hot chocolate and something to eat on their sleigh ride.'

Lucas raised an eyebrow. 'How did you know?'

Sofia smiled and shrugged. 'You're a soft touch.'

'All right,' he asked the girls, 'who would like a lift home in the sleigh?'

'Really?'

'Yep.'

His offer was met with a chorus of squeals and as Banjo had finished all the apples that were on offer to him Lucas helped the girls into the sleigh before climbing up to sit on the driver's seat beside François.

The sleigh had been decorated with pine wreaths, bells and ribbons, and François had also decorated Banjo's harness with bells and tinsel. The shake of his head as he started to pull the sleigh set the bells ringing. Lucas asked François to take them for a turn around the plaza before heading to the patisserie. He'd acquiesced on the ride as he wanted a chance to chat to Lily, wanted to find out what she knew about Australia, but sitting up next to François while Lily sat in the back wasn't going to get him the answers he wanted.

He delivered Annabel and Claire to their mother and told Fleur that he would take Lily to collect Jess.

'Banjo can take you to your mum's work, Lily. Would you like to sit up front next to François?' Lucas asked, and when Lily nodded he lifted her onto the driver's seat. This seat was higher than the passenger seat to allow François to see over Banjo, and the position afforded Lily an uninterrupted view of the Village. The sun had set and the streets and the plaza were glowing under the Christmas lights. Lucas grabbed a fur blanket from the back of the sleigh and tucked it over Lily's lap.

On the seat next to them was the cardboard box Sofia had given him. Lucas peeked inside. Sofia had packed some pieces of cake and Lucas's favourite chocolate biscuits. The girls had finished their hot drinks but hadn't had time to eat anything. He showed the contents of the box to Lily as Banjo set off again, pulling the sleigh through the snow. 'Would you like a piece of cake?'

'No, thank you, I don't really like cake.'

'How about chocolate biscuits, then? I know you like chocolate.'

'How do you know that?'

'Who doesn't like chocolate? And these are the best chocolate biscuits ever. I get them sent over to me from Australia,' he told her.

'Really?' she asked, as she picked one up and bit into it.

'Do you like it?'

Lily nodded.

'So that's something you know about Australia—we make good chocolate biscuits. Tell me what else you know.'

'I know about the animals.'

'Do you have a favourite?'

Lily nodded again. 'Mum says I remind her of a platypus but I like the koala best,' she said with a mouthful of chocolate biscuit, 'because it's so cute. I know what the flag looks like too but I like our flag better. Did you know you've got the same queen as us?'

'I did know that.' Lucas smiled. She really was adorable.

'I can sing "Kookaburra sits in the old gum tree".'

'Did your mum teach you?'

'No, I learnt it in school. Mum taught me "Waltzing Matilda".'

Lucas remembered teaching that song to Jess and explaining what all the words meant. Why had Jess told Lily so much about Australia? 'Did you know that in

Australia it's summertime now? It's so hot at Christ-mastime we all go to the beach for a swim.'

'That's silly. Who would want to go to the beach on Christmas?'

'Yeah, you're right.' Lucas had come to love a white Christmas but that might be because it reminded him of Jess. It was far more romantic to think of cuddling by a warm fire with snow falling outside than sweating under a blazing sun, battling flies and sand. He loved summer but he didn't have to have it at Christmastime.

Lucas checked his watch. It was almost five. 'We'd better get you to the medical centre,' he told Lily. 'Your mum will be finishing work soon and I promised Fleur I would have you there on time.'

'Oh.' Lily pouted. 'Is that the end of my sleigh ride?'

'I have an idea. Does your mum like surprises?'

Lily nodded. 'She likes good surprises. She says I was a good surprise.'

'Excellent. Why don't we go and pick her up from work in the sleigh? Do you think she'd like that?'

Lily nodded, her green eyes wide.

'That's healed up nicely, Oscar,' Jess said as she re-moved the stitches in the chin of a teenage boy. He had come off second best in a tussle between the snow-boarding half-pipe and his board and Jess had assisted Cameron when he'd fixed him up a week earlier. She snipped the last stitch and pulled it from the skin. 'See if you can stay out of trouble now, won't you?' Oscar was a regular visitor to the clinic and Jess suspected his skills on his snowboard didn't quite match up to his enthusiasm.

'I'll try,' he said, as he hopped up from the examination bed. 'But maybe I should make a time for next week just in case I need it.'

'I don't want to see you again for at least two weeks.' She laughed. 'Off you go.'

Oscar was her last patient for the evening and she checked her watch as she typed his notes into the computer. She was finishing on time and was looking forward to collecting Lily from Fleur's and getting home. Sliding her arms into her coat, she switched off the computer and pulled the door closed as she prepared to leave for the day. Heading into the reception area to say goodnight to Donna, she was surprised to find Lily there.

'Hi, Lil, what are you doing here?' She frowned as she bent down to give her daughter a kiss.

'We have a surprise for you.'

'We?'

Lily took her hand and led her outside. Lucas was standing on the porch.

He looked gorgeous. He was wearing a grey cashmere coat that contrasted nicely with his forget-me-not-blue eyes. His coat looked smart and expensive. Her own coat was several years old and Jess was well aware of the contrast in their wardrobes.

'Lucas,' she greeted him.

'Hello, JJ.' He smiled at her and her heart beat a tattoo in her chest.

She hadn't seen him for a week and the sight of him took her breath away all over again. How was it possible that she could forget the effect his smile had on her? It was like seeing the sun coming out when she hadn't noticed it was missing. She'd never thought her day needed brightening until Lucas had popped into it.

But that didn't explain what he was doing there. In front of her work. With her daughter. Lily didn't know Lucas. He didn't know Lily. She had deliberately kept them apart. She didn't want him getting to know Lily. Not until she'd decided what to do. So what on earth were they doing together? What was going on?

'Why are you here?' she asked. 'Why are you *both* here?'

'Lily went walkabout.'

'What's walkabout?' Lily wanted to know.

Lucas looked at Lily as he explained. 'It's something we say in Australia. It means you went wandering.'

'What? Where?' Jess was worried. She had wanted Lily to be able to roam around the village safely, she'd felt confident that it would be possible, but she realised now that she'd assumed Lily would be wandering with her permission. Not taking off on a whim whenever the mood struck her. 'Did you find her?'

'No.' Lucas was shaking his head. 'She came to the lodge.'

'Why? What for?' Why would Lily go to Lucas? Jess turned to her daughter. 'Lily, what's going on?' She could hear the note of panic in her voice but there was nothing she could do to stop it.

'Jess, it's all right.'

Lucas's voice was calm, his words measured. He was always very calm, very matter-of-fact and practical. A whole lot of personality traits that Jess was sure she could use but it wasn't his place to placate her.

'Don't tell me it's all right!' she hissed at him.

'Lily, Banjo looks hungry.' Lucas turned to Lily, ignoring Jess's outburst. 'Why don't you go and ask François if he has another apple that you can give him?'

Jess watched as Lily went down the steps at the front of the clinic to where the Crystal Lodge sleigh was waiting in the snow. She hadn't even noticed it she'd been so distracted by Lucas and Lily arriving on her doorstep. She assumed Banjo was the horse, a very large but fortunately placid-looking horse.

Once Lily was out of earshot Lucas turned back to Jess. 'Lily was quite safe. I thought this was what you wanted—for her to be able to feel safe in the village?'

'Within reason,' Jess snapped. 'I didn't expect her to roam the streets alone or take off without notice.' Who knew what might happen? All Jess's insecurities, deeply embedded into her psyche by her parents, came to the fore.

'Is this about Stephen?' Lucas asked. He was watching her carefully with his gorgeous eyes. Was he waiting to see if she was going to explode with anger or dissolve into tears?

Jess had to admit that in a way it did all relate back to her brother. She nodded. 'I wanted Lily to have the freedom I never had but I expected to know where she was. She's too young to be getting about on her own. She'd supposed to have someone with her.'

'She wasn't alone. Annabel and Claire were with her. Claire was supposed to be taking them ice skating.'

'So what happened? How did Lily end up with you?'

Lucas shrugged. 'She wanted a sleigh ride so I gather she convinced Annabel to take off with her and they came to the lodge to see if they could use their ice-skating money for a ride instead.' he said, as if that was a perfectly natural request to make of a complete stranger.

'And you said yes, I see.' Jess was annoyed. Not only had Lily gone and found Lucas, she'd also managed to wangle a sleigh ride out of him. She'd been planning that as a holiday surprise and Lucas had taken that gift away from her. She knew it wasn't his fault—he hadn't done it deliberately—but it still irked her.

'I did clear it with Fleur first,' he told her. 'You should be proud of Lily. She wanted something badly enough to go after it. That shows initiative, determination and commitment, and I thought she deserved to be rewarded.'

He would think that, Jess thought, even though she knew her bitchy attitude was unfair.

'And I didn't think you'd mind, especially if you got to share it with her.'

'What do you mean?'

'We've come to give you a lift home in the sleigh. We thought we'd take the long way around. What do you say? Am I forgiven?' He held his hands out, palms open, beseeching her, and she couldn't stay mad. She knew she shouldn't be cross with him anyway, he had only been trying to do something nice for Lily and for her.

And he was right. Did it matter that she hadn't organised it? She should be happy. Lily was safe and she was getting her treat. And it wasn't costing her anything. Well, not money at least. It was costing her some pride and now she would owe Lucas a favour.

He smiled at her. His dimples flashed and his blue eyes twinkled. She would owe him a favour, but when he smiled at her she figured she could live with that.

She sighed. 'I'm sorry I snapped at you. And, yes, you're forgiven.'

'Good. Shall we?' He bent his elbow and Jess tucked her hand into the crook of his arm as he led her down the steps to the sleigh. She put one foot onto the running board and felt Lucas's hands on her hips as he helped her up. She sank into the soft leather seat as Lucas lifted Lily up beside her. He climbed in on the other side of Lily and tucked rugs around them all.

François clicked his tongue at Banjo and the big horse moved off slowly, bells jingling.

'Mummy, I can't see,' Lily complained.

She was tucked between Jess and Lucas and was too small to see past them or over the front of the sleigh.

'Hold up, please, François, while we do some reshuffling,' Lucas said.

Lily and Jess swapped seats so Lily could see out of the side of the sleigh but this meant that Jess was now sitting beside Lucas. Their knees were touching under the blanket and Jess was very aware of the heat of his body radiating across to her. He took up a lot of space and she could have shifted closer to Lily to give them both some room but she didn't want to. It felt good to sit this close to him.

'How has your week been?' he asked, as Banjo set off again.

'It was busy. Apparently the resort is almost at full capacity, I suppose you know that, but we also really notice the influx of the tourists as we get an increase in patient load.'

'Do you still think you've made the right choice taking this job?'

'Definitely. It's so much better than my old job in so many ways. No shift work, no weekends. Three minutes from home. It's heaven.'

'What are your plans for the weekend?'

'I'm not sure. Nothing much. We'll probably do a bit of skiing. Lily has been having lessons after school so I like to see how she's progressing. She's been pestering me for a sleigh ride since we arrived in Moose River but I won't need to do that now.' She smiled at him, all traces of her earlier irritation having vanished. The sleigh ride was relaxing and romantic, even with Lily in tow. It was a lovely end to the working week and sitting beside Lucas was the icing on the cake. 'Thank you.'

'My pleasure.'

She could see his forget-me-not-blue eyes shining in the light of the streetlamps. He looked very pleased with himself. As he had every right to be.

He was humming carols—something about it being lovely weather for a sleigh ride together—as François took them on a circuit around the village. Lucas's hand found hers under the blanket. He squeezed it gently and didn't let go.

Jess rested her head on his shoulder. She didn't stop to think about what she was doing. It just felt natural. It felt good. Banjo headed up the hill where François stopped to let them take in the view of the village, which was spread out before them. The lights sparkled and danced and the sounds of happiness drifted up to them on the breeze. Jess sighed. Sitting in the sleigh, listening to Lucas humming, and seeing Lily's smile, she imagined this could be what her life would be like if they were a real family. Cocooned in their own little bubble of contentment.

She suspected that anyone looking at them now would assume that's what they were. A blond family, bundled up in their furs, being pulled through the snow on a sleigh. They could be the perfect image on a festive season card.

Only it wasn't the truth.

Lucas wasn't her reality. He wasn't her Prince Charming.

She still didn't know if he even wanted a family.

Telling him everything might ruin it all.

Banjo had begun picking his way back down the hill and within minutes François had guided him to a stop in front of her apartment block. It was late now. It was time for dinner.

Lucas helped them down from the sleigh and walked them to the door.

'I know you have other priorities and I don't want you to feel as though I'm intruding on your life, but I would really like to spend some time with you. With you and Lily,' he said, as he held the door open. 'Tomorrow evening is the first Christmas market for the season and we're switching on the lights on the Christmas tree out the front of the lodge. I'd like the two of you to be my guests for the tree lighting. What do you think?'

Jess thought she should refuse politely but she couldn't. She wanted to see him too and Lily would love it.

If Lily and Lucas wanted something badly enough, they would both go after it. That was definitely a trait of nature, not nurture, but why shouldn't she do the same? She and Lily could spend time with Lucas, it would give her another chance to see how he interacted with Lily, another chance to watch him. Was it her fault if having Lily there meant she had to hold onto her secret for one more day?

'We'd love to,' she said. 'Thank you.'

CHAPTER EIGHT

THE THIRTY-FOOT FIR tree stood sentinel over the plaza. Lily craned her head to see to the very top where the star was perched, and even Jess looked up in awe. She'd noticed the framework being erected—that had been difficult to miss too—but the tree itself, with its spreading limbs, was simply enormous. Its dark green foliage had been decorated with myriad silver balls and shining stars and bells that rang when the breeze stirred the branches. A light, shaped like a candle, was attached to the end of each branch. It must have taken hours to decorate but the effort was well worth it. It was beautiful.

Lucas came to them as they stood under the tree. He had his grey cashmere overcoat on again with a black scarf wrapped around his throat. Jess had made more of an attempt to dress up tonight. She'd chosen her smartest woollen coat in a winter white and had taken time with her make-up.

'Ladies, your timing is perfect.' Lucas greeted them with a smile and Jess was pleased she'd made the extra effort.

Lucas had reserved a table for them on the outdoor dining terrace in front of the lodge. They had an uninterrupted view across to the tree as well as down to the plaza, where the colourful tented market stalls had been set up. Carol singers were performing at the edge of the terrace and Lucas ordered eggnog for everyone as they sat down.

As the eggnog was served Lily handed Lucas a box wrapped in Christmas ribbon.

'What's this for?'

'For you,' Lily told him. 'To say thank you for the sleigh ride.'

Lucas undid the ribbon and lifted the lid to reveal cookies in various Christmas shapes—stars, angels, reindeer, bells and sleighs. Each cookie had been decorated with icing and had a small hole in the top through which red ribbon had been threaded.

'Mum and I made gingerbread for the school Christmas cookie swap and I thought you might like some.'

'Thank you, Lily, they look delicious,' he said, as he lifted out a star.

'You can't eat them yet!' Lily admonished him. 'You're supposed to hang them on the tree. That's why they've got ribbons in them.'

'I see that now. Have you hung some on your tree?'

'We don't have a tree.'

'You don't?'

'I haven't got around to it,' Jess told him. She wasn't actually planning on having a tree, mainly because she didn't have any decorations for it. She hadn't brought decorations with them to Moose River—that hadn't seemed a necessity when she'd been choosing which belongings needed to fit into their luggage—but now that she was immersed in the festive spirit of the village she regretted her decision. It wasn't likely to change, though. She could get a tree but she still didn't have the money to splash out on new decorations. Of course, she wasn't about to tell Lucas that. Fortunately Lily piped up and redirected the conversation.

'Do you have a Christmas tree inside?' she asked.

'I do,' Lucas replied.

'I think you should hang them inside, then, so they don't get snowed on.'

'I think that's a very good idea.'

The carol singers were singing 'O Christmas Tree' and as they neared the end of the song Lucas stood up.

'That's my cue,' he said. 'Would you like to come with me, Lily? We need to start the countdown for the lights.'

He took Lily's hand and a lump formed in Jess's throat as she watched the two of them make their way to the tree. He was being so sweet with her. She didn't know what she was worried about. He would love Lily.

Actually, she did know what she was worried about. She was worried he'd think less of her for keeping the secret. She didn't want that but there was no way around it. She knew she had to tell him the truth. She just hadn't decided when.

Lucas took a cordless microphone from his pocket and switched it on. He looked confident and relaxed and very sexy.

'Welcome everyone to the inaugural lighting of the Crystal Lodge Christmas tree. I'd like to invite you all to help count us down from ten to one before we flick the switch. Lily, would you like to start us off?'

Lily looked up at Lucas and beamed. Jess thought her smile was so wide it was going to split her face in two. She was looking at Lucas as if he was the best thing that had ever happened to her, and Jess knew Lily would only benefit from having Lucas as a father. There would be no downside for Lily. Jess had to do the right thing.

Lucas handed Lily the microphone. 'Ready? From ten.'

'Ten!' Lily's voice rang out across the plaza and then the crowd joined in.

'Nine, eight, seven, six, five, four, three, two, one!'

As they reached 'one', the lights were switched on, accompanied by a massive cheer. The tips of the candle lights were illuminated and now glowed brightly against the night sky. The tree had a light dusting of snow and looked magical.

As the carol singers launched into another set of carols Lucas and Lily returned to their table.

'Did you see that, Mum?'

Jess had tears in her eyes as she got out of her chair and hugged her very excited daughter. 'I did, darling, you were fabulous.' Over the top of Lily's head she mouthed 'Thank you' to Lucas.

'Can we go to the market now?' Lily asked, and Jess knew she wasn't going to be able to sit still.

'Would you like to come with us or are you busy?' she invited Lucas.

'No, my duties are all done for the evening. I'd love to walk with you.'

They strolled through the market, stopping at any stall that caught their attention. There was a good variety selling food and gifts, everything from scarves, knitted hats and delicate glassware to souvenirs, Christmas decorations, hot food and candies.

Lucas stopped at a stall selling decorations. 'Lily, I think I need a few more decorations for my inside trees, to go with your cookies. Would you like to choose some for me?'

Lily agonised over her choices but eventually had filled a bag with a varied assortment of ornaments. Jess wasn't sure how they would match in with the smartly decorated trees in the lodge's lobby but seeing the pleasure on Lily's face she knew that wasn't the point. Lucas was doing all sorts of wonderful things for Lily that Jess couldn't afford to do but she couldn't begrudge him. Not when she could see how much pleasure Lily was getting from it.

Jess stopped at the next stall, which was selling barley candy. This was a Canadian Christmas tradition and one she could afford. It was also one she'd shared with Lucas years ago. She chose three sticks of the sugary sweets, one shaped like Santa, one a Christmas tree and the third a reindeer, and let Lily and Lucas choose one each.

They sucked on the candy as they wandered through the market. Lily skipped in front of them, in a hurry to see what lay in the stalls ahead. She stopped at one that displayed some intricate doll's houses, complete with delicate furniture and real glass windows, and spent ages admiring the display as Lucas and Jess talked.

'What are your plans for Christmas?' Lucas asked. 'Are your parents coming up to the resort?'

Jess shook her head. 'I don't think so.'

'Really? I thought that was a family tradition for you?'

Jess had no idea what her parents' plans were. They could be spending Christmas here but even if they were their celebration wouldn't include her and she wasn't going to explain why that tradition had come to an end.

She stopped to buy a bag of hot cinnamon doughnut holes, hoping that would distract him from any further questions.

'What about you?' she asked, as Lily traded her barley sugar for the bag of doughnuts.

'I'll be hosting the Christmas lunch at the lodge. A buffet extravaganza.'

'A bit different from your traditional Christmas,' she said.

'I've grown to prefer a white Christmas.' Lucas smiled. 'It feels more like a celebration to me.'

They had reached the ice-skating rink at the end of the first row of market stalls and they sat on a bench to eat doughnut holes and watch the ice skaters. Lily leant on the railing, leaving Jess and Lucas free to talk. Jess sat at one end of the bench, which was a long bench with plenty of room, but Lucas chose to sit right next to her.

'What has Lily asked Santa for?'

'It's the same thing every year, a baby sister.'

'I take it from your tone you have no plans to give her what she wants.' He was smiling.

Jess shook her head. 'I'm not doing that again. Not on my own.'

Lily came back to Jess and handed her the empty doughnut bag. 'Can we go ice skating?' she asked.

'I guess so.' Jess knew it was only a few dollars to hire the skates.

'I might have to sit this one out. I'm a terrible ice skater. I'm Australian, remember, there's not much ice where I come from.'

Disappointment flowed through Jess. She hadn't stopped to think that this might be something Lucas wouldn't enjoy. But, taking a leaf out of his book, she decided persistence might pay off. 'Lily and I will help you,' she suggested. 'We can hold your hands.'

Lucas flashed his dimples at her as he grinned and said, 'There's an offer too good to refuse. Let's do it.'

He scooped Lily up and she squealed with delight as he carried her over to the hire kiosk to choose skates. It seemed his charm worked equally as well on Lily as it did on her.

Jess tied Lily's skates and then she and Lily each took one of Lucas's hands and stepped onto the ice. Lucas struggled to get the idea of gliding on the slippery surface but his innate sense of balance meant she and Lily had no trouble keeping him upright as they skated around the rink.

They'd managed to negotiate their way twice around the rink before Lily saw one of her friends from school and skated off, leaving Jess alone with Lucas.

'Did you want to keep skating?' she asked him.

'Definitely,' he replied. 'I'm not going to pass up an opportunity to have you all to myself.' He pulled his gloves off his hands and put them into his pocket. He held out his hand and Jess slipped her gloves off too and gave them to him before putting her hand in his outstretched palm. His skin was warm but Jess knew she wouldn't care how cold it got, she wasn't going to put her gloves back on.

They did a couple more laps of the rink hand in hand and then Lucas let her go.

'Are you going to try by yourself?' she asked.

'No,' he said, as he put his arm around her waist and pulled her in closer. 'I still need to lean on you.'

Jess knew that was a bad idea—he wasn't steady enough on his skates yet—but before she could protest he'd pushed off and within a few feet their skates had tangled. Lucas stumbled and grabbed the railing that ran around the edge of the rink and just managed to keep his feet, but his momentum as he tried to regain his balance spun Jess around so that she was now facing him. They leant together on the railing as Lucas straightened up.

He was laughing. 'Sorry about that,' he said. 'Actually, I'm not sorry, it's put you right where I want you.'

She was almost nose to nose with Lucas and she could feel her cheeks burning but it wasn't from the cold. It was from being so close to him. Jess lifted her chin and looked into his forget-me-not-blue eyes. She could feel his breath on her cheek. Warm and sweet, it smelt of cinnamon doughnuts. She was close enough to kiss him.

Lucas dipped his head. She knew what he was going to do. But she couldn't let him kiss her. Not here. Not yet. But she couldn't move away. She was transfixed by his eyes. She held her breath as she watched his eyes darken from blue to purple as he closed the distance.

Jess felt something tugging on her coat.

'Mummy, I feel sick.'

Jess looked down. Lily was beside her. 'Lily? What's the matter?'

'I feel sick,' she repeated.

Was she dizzy from skating? Jess wondered. She did look a bit pale. Jess let go of Lucas to put her hand on Lily's forehead. She felt warm but Jess found it hard to tell if that was just because of all the layers she was bundled up in.

'Too much sugar, probably,' Jess said. 'We'd better get you home.'

'I can't walk,' Lily grumbled.

'I'll give you a piggyback,' Lucas offered, and Jess looked at him gratefully.

Lily didn't need to be asked twice. She whipped her skates off, pulled her boots back on and wasted no time hopping onto Lucas's back, where she held on tight and buried her face in his neck as he carried her home.

'You're making a habit of getting us home safely,' Jess said, as Lucas put Lily onto the couch.

'I'm happy to be of service,' he said with a smile. 'Are you going to be all right?'

'We'll be fine. Thank you.' It wasn't quite the ending she'd pictured to the night but there wasn't anything she could do about that.

Jess was browning onions to add to the meatballs she was planning to make when there was a knock on the apartment door. 'Can you answer that, please, Lily?'

'Who is it?' she called out to Lily as she heard the door open.

'It's a Christmas tree!'

Jess wiped her hands on a tea towel and stepped out of the kitchen. A pine tree filled the doorway. 'What on earth…?'

Lucas's face appeared around the side of the tree. He was grinning at Lily. 'G'day.'

'Lucas!' Lily jumped up and down and clapped her hands as she shouted. All trace of yesterday's illness had well and truly disappeared. 'Who's the tree for?'

'You. I thought it might cheer you up if you were sick but you look like you're feeling much better.'

'I am better but, please, can I still have it? I *love* Christmas trees, they're so pretty.'

'It's not pretty yet but it will be once we decorate it.'

'That's very sweet of you,' Jess interrupted before the excitement took over completely, 'but I haven't got time to be fiddling around with a tree.'

'What's the problem?' Lucas asked, as he leant the tree against the door frame and stepped into the apartment.

He looked as disappointed as Jess knew Lily would be but as much as she would have loved to have a Christmas tree she hadn't the budget for one. She'd thought about decorating the room with a small pine bough and maybe spending an afternoon making kissing balls with Lily as a compromise, but that was as far as she'd got. 'It's always so difficult to get it secure and then in a couple of weeks I'll just have to work out how to get rid of a dead tree.'

'That's why I'm here. I will make sure it won't topple over and I promise I will dispose of it when you're ready. All you need to do is tell me where you'd like it.'

'Lucas, have a look.' Jess waved an arm around at the cramped living space. 'There's nowhere for it to go.'

'Why don't I put it in front of the balcony doors? How much time do you spend out there in this weather anyway?'

He smiled at her and Jess remembered how it had been when she'd been seventeen. She would have given him the world when he'd smiled at her. She had. And she thought she still might.

But she wasn't ready to give in just yet. 'I like to look at the village lights,' she protested.

'How about, for the next three weeks, you look at the lights on the tree instead?'

He made a fair point but she didn't have any decorations and that included lights. 'I don't—'

'Have lights,' Lucas interrupted. 'No dramas. I do. I have everything you need. Just say yes.'

Did he have everything she needed? Should she say yes? It was a tempting offer.

'Please, Mum?'

Why was she refusing? She'd dreamt of giving Lily a perfect Christmas and Lucas was here, offering to help make that happen. She'd offer him one last chance to excuse himself. 'I'm sure you've got better things to do too,' she said to Lucas.

'Nope. It's Sunday. I'm taking the day off. This'll be relaxing.'

Jess laughed. 'You think? Why don't you go out snowboarding? Wouldn't that be more fun?'

'It'll be snowing for the next four months, there's plenty of time for that. Christmas is in three weeks, which makes this a priority.'

She couldn't resist a combined assault. 'All right, if you're sure.' She gave in. 'But you and Lily will have to manage without me. I've got a mountain of mincemeat waiting to be turned into dinner.'

'No worries. We'll be right, won't we, Lily?'

Lily nodded her head eagerly.

Jess would actually have loved to help but she'd already said she didn't have time. But Lucas didn't argue—he didn't seem to mind at all, leaving Jess feeling mildly disappointed. Had he only come to see Lily?

Lucas tossed his coat onto the sofa and then Lily helped him to carry all the paraphernalia into the apartment. He'd brought everything they would need, including all the decorations Lily had bought at the market the day before plus candy canes and some of the gingerbread. The tree was only small, maybe a touch over five feet tall, and Jess had to admit it was perfect for the compact apartment.

Jess watched out of the corner of her eye, unable to resist an opportunity to watch Lucas. She forgot all about the onions on the stove as she watched his arms flex and his T-shirt strain across his shoulders as he hefted the tree inside and fitted it into the stand.

The smell of burning onions eventually returned her focus to the kitchen and she pitched the singed batch and chopped a second lot as Lucas and Lily trimmed the tree. He had even brought Christmas music—Jess could hear it playing on his phone while they worked.

'What are you listening to?' she asked.

He named a well-known Australian children's group. 'This is their Christmas album.'

'Why do you have their music?'

'I downloaded it for Lily. I thought she'd enjoy it,' he explained. 'Surely you recognise the songs, even if you're not familiar with the artists?'

'I will by the end of the afternoon,' Jess quipped. 'You seem to have it stuck on repeat.'

Lucas laughed and the sound filled the space. It was a lovely sound, better than the music, and Jess wished she could hear that whenever she liked.

'We like it, don't we, Lily?'

'Yes, it's fun.'

Jess felt even more left out as she listened to them laugh and sing along to Lucas's music. But she'd had six years of having Lily to herself. It was time Lily got to know Lucas.

But was she ready to share? What implications would

it have? He said he'd come back for her but what if he changed his mind? What if he only wanted Lily? What if he wanted to take her away? What was best for Lily? Should she turn her world upside down? Could Lucas give her things that she couldn't?

She knew he could.

He already had.

The tree was finished and Lily had switched the lights on. It looked very pretty and lifted Jess's spirits. 'Would you like to stay for dinner?' she invited Lucas. 'We're having spaghetti with meatballs.'

'I don't want to be rude but I don't eat pasta.'

'Oh.' Her heart dropped. It seemed he didn't want to spend time with her.

'Would it be all right if I just had the meatballs?'

'I don't want spaghetti either,' Lily said, but Jess wasn't all that surprised. Lucas was Lily's new idol so, of course, she'd want to imitate him. She hadn't stopped talking about him all day and it had almost been a relief when he'd arrived at their door. At least then Jess hadn't had to listen to Lily's running commentary any more, but having Lucas there in the flesh had added other frustrations. She could see him and smell his winter-fresh pine scent but she couldn't touch him.

Lucas and Lily sat opposite Jess with their bowls of meatballs sprinkled with cheese. Jess could see some similarities. Lily may look just like her but her green eyes were more changeable. Tonight, sitting next to Lucas, Jess could see that flash of forget-me-not blue in them. It was odd that she'd never noticed that before.

Looking at them sitting opposite her, Jess had an-other glimpse of what it would be like to be a family, and she wondered what Lucas would say if she told him the truth tonight.

But she couldn't tell him in front of Lily. Despite how he'd treated Lily over the past couple of days, she couldn't assume that his reaction would be positive. Being nice to an old friend's daughter was one thing, finding out he was a father might be another thing entirely. Jess couldn't risk upsetting Lily if Lucas's reaction wasn't what she hoped. This wasn't a conversation she could launch into on the spur of the moment. They needed time alone, without interruption. She needed a plan.

Perhaps she should ask Fleur if Lily could have a sleepover with Annabel. She didn't like to ask for favours but given the circumstances it was probably her best option. Either that or get Kristie to come up to the resort to babysit. Kristie had been right. Lucas deserved to know the truth.

Christmas was fast approaching and Lily's calendar was chock-full of activities, far more so than Jess's was. In the past week alone she'd had the Christmas cookie swap, a Christmas lunch, yesterday had been Annabel's birthday party and tonight she was supposed to be going back to Annabel's for a sleepover, but right now it didn't look as though that was going to happen.

Lily had started vomiting after the party and fifteen hours later she hadn't stopped and Jess was beginning to worry. She called the clinic for advice as she spooned ice chips into Lily's mouth. She tried to think what she would advise a stressed parent in this situation if she was the nurse who took the call, but sleep deprivation and worry made it difficult to think clearly.

Donna answered the clinic phone and put her straight through to Cameron.

Jess explained the situation and Lily's symptoms. 'She's been vomiting since four o'clock yesterday, she's complaining of abdominal pain—that's not unusual but she's extremely lethargic.'

'Do you think it could be her appendix?'

Jess had thought about that but Lily's symptoms didn't fit and she'd just assumed it was a usual childhood stomach ache, which Lily seemed to get plenty of, but what if it was more serious than that?

'I've checked but what if I've missed something?'

'I'll come over as soon as I can.'

Jess sat with Lily and fretted while she waited for Cameron. This was one of the things she hated about being a single parent. There was no one to share the worry with.

'Has she had a temperature overnight?' Cameron asked when he arrived.

'No.'

'No, not now or, no, not at any stage?' Cameron clarified.

'Not at any point.'

'Any urine output in the last four to six hours?'

'No.'

'When was her last bowel movement?'

'Yesterday?' Jess wasn't one hundred per cent sure.

Cameron examined Lily and checked for signs of appendicitis. 'I agree with you. I don't think it's her appendix. How quickly did she get sick after the party?'

'Pretty quick. A couple of hours.'

'Too soon for it to be food poisoning. And no one else has had any gastro?'

Jess shook her head. She'd spoken to Fleur and between the two of them they'd rung and checked with the other parents.

Cameron motioned for Jess to follow him out of the bedroom. 'I think it would be best to take her down to the hospital. They should run some tests. She could have a bowel obstruction but she'll need an X-ray to check that out.'

'A bowel obstruction!' That was not good news.

'It's one possibility and I think it should be investigated. The hospital will be able to run blood tests and get the results faster than I can up here on the mountain. I can treat her for dehydration but that's treating the symptoms, not the cause. Would you like Ellen to drive you? She's not working today.'

'Thanks, but I'll call a friend.' Jess didn't want to impose on Cameron or his wife any more than necessary. She had made plans to have dinner with Lucas tonight and it looked like she was going to have to call him to cancel but she hoped he would offer to drive them down the mountain. 'If he can't take us, I'll call Ellen.'

'All right, I'll let the hospital know to expect you.'

Just as she'd hoped, Lucas offered to drive them. She'd rather he was with her than Ellen. They were both busy and probably neither had the time to spend being her taxi service but Lucas had more invested in Lily—he just didn't know it yet.

Lily didn't vomit at all on the hour-long trip to the hospital, which Jess was grateful for. Lucas dropped them at the entrance to the emergency department and went to park the car. The hospital was small. At the bottom of the mountain it was still more than an hour out of Vancouver, but it did have modern facilities. Jess carried Lily inside and walked straight up to the desk.

'This is Lily Johnson. Dr Cameron Baker was calling ahead for us.'

The nurse on duty took them straight into a partitioned cubicle. There wasn't a lot of privacy but Jess knew most patients in an emergency department had bigger priorities than to be fussing about privacy. Jess ran through all Lily's symptoms with the nurse while she took Lily's obs and then listened as the nurse repeated them to the doctor, who had introduced himself as Peter Davis.

'This is Lily. Age six, weight sixteen kilograms. She has been vomiting since yesterday afternoon but nothing for the past two hours. Complaining of stomach pains. Afebrile. BP normal. No diarrhoea.'

'Current temperature?'

'Thirty-seven point two.'

'No allergies?' He looked at Jess.

'No,' she replied.

'What has she eaten?'

'Nothing since yesterday afternoon.'

'What did she eat yesterday?'

'I don't really know. She went to a party but none of the other children are sick, I checked.' Jess knew the doctor was thinking about food poisoning as one option.

'Has there been any gastro at the school?'

'No. Nothing.'

'No major illnesses? No surgeries?'

Jess shook her head again.

'Any episodes of rumbling appendix?' Peter continued to question her.

'No, and her GP didn't seem to think it was her appendix. He thought she could have a bowel obstruction.'

Jess was getting distressed. She didn't want to tell the doctor what to look for—she knew there was a routine, she knew he would want to eliminate more common possibilities first, and there was no need to run unnecessary tests if Lily's problem was something simple, but she wanted to make sure he didn't miss anything or ignore something more significant. A bowel obstruction could be nasty and Jess really hoped it wasn't the case but nothing else seemed to fit.

'No diarrhoea, you said?' he asked as he conducted the rebound test, checking for appendicitis.

'No.'

'Can you cough for me, Lily?'

Lily coughed obediently and didn't show any signs of discomfort.

'Is there any past history of recurrent diarrhoea or blood in her stools?'

'No.'

'I'll run a drip to counteract her dehydration and organise an abdominal X-ray. See if that can shed any light on the situation.'

Jess held Lily's hand as the nurse inserted a canula and connected a drip. Lily was very flat but that might have been related to lack of sleep. Jess wasn't feeling so bright herself.

The nurse fixed a drip stand to a wheelchair and helped Lily into the seat, explaining she would take her over to the radiology department. Jess walked beside the wheelchair and tried to keep a positive frame of mind, but it was difficult when she could see Lily so pale and quiet, with needles and tubes sticking out of her.

Jess waited as the X-ray was taken. Then she waited for the result.

'The X-ray was inconclusive,' Dr Davis told her. 'We'll do a CT scan next but I'm not sure we're looking in the right place.'

'What do you mean?' Jess was confused.

'Her pain has eased considerably and she's stopped vomiting. I don't think it's all as a result of the medication. I think she may have purged her system of whatever was upsetting her. Has she *ever* had any allergy testing done?'

Jess shook her head.

'Is there any family history of allergies or gastro-intestinal problems?'

'She's a fussy eater with the usual childhood stomach aches but no allergies that I know of.'

'Any auto-immune deficiencies?'

'Not on my side, but I'm not sure about her father's side.' It was obvious that the tests weren't giving the doctor the answers he was expecting but Jess didn't have any other answers for him. She would have to talk to Lucas. She had to know what was wrong with Lily and Lucas could hold the key. 'I'll see what I can find out,' she said.

Knowing Lily wouldn't be able to see her while she was in the CT scanner, Jess returned to the waiting room to see if Lucas had appeared. She needed to find him. She needed answers. The time had come. She had secrets that needed to be told.

He was in the waiting room when she returned. He stood up when she walked in and came towards her with his arms open. She stepped into his embrace.

'How're you doing?' he asked. 'How's Lily? Do they know what's wrong?'

'They're still not sure. The doctor was thinking appendicitis or a small bowel obstruction but the X-ray was inconclusive. They're doing a CT scan now but the doctor seems to be leaning towards an allergy of some sort. He was asking about her family history but, of course, I only know half of the answers.'

'Well, there's not much you can do about that,' Lucas said, 'unless you can track down Lily's father.'

Jess took a deep breath. The time had come. 'I have,' she told him.

'What? Have you spoken to him?'

'Yes and no. Will you come outside with me? I need some fresh air.' She knew she had some explaining to do but she wasn't about to go into the details in the middle of the emergency department. Jess stepped out through the automatic sliding door. There was a bench just outside. She sat and waited until Lucas was sitting beside her.

It was time.

'I know where Lily's father is,' she said. She took another deep breath. 'It's you. You're her father.'

CHAPTER NINE

'WHAT?' LUCAS SHOT straight back up off the bench as if it was electrified. 'What the hell are you saying?'

'Lily is your daughter.'

'What? No. She can't be.'

Jess nodded. 'You're her father.'

'She's mine?' He shook his head in disbelief. 'I have a daughter?'

Lucas paced backwards and forwards in front of the bench while Jess waited nervously. What was going through his head?

He stopped and looked at her, a puzzled expression in his forget-me-not-blue eyes. 'You're sure about this?'

'Of course I'm sure.'

'But why haven't you told me?' Lucas stood in front of her, rooted to the spot. He ran his hands through his hair and stared at her with a fixed, unseeing expression. 'How could you keep this from me? *Why* would you keep this from me?'

'I'm sorry.'

'What for?' He was looking at her now, his blue eyes boring into her as if he was searching for any more secrets she had yet to divulge. 'For telling me? For not telling me? For keeping her a secret? Which one of those things are you apologising for?'

Jess felt ill. She swallowed nervously and she could taste bile in her throat. 'I'm sorry for telling you the way I did. I didn't mean to blurt it out like that.'

'How could you have kept this a secret?'

'I didn't mean to. I tried to find you.'

'When?'

'When I found out I was pregnant. Kristie and I hired a private investigator but after a month the PI told us we were wasting our time. Do you know how many Lucas Whites there are in Australia? And not one of them was you.'

'When was this?'

'It was April. The ski season was over, the resort had closed for the summer and you would have been home in Australia.'

Lucas's legs folded and he sat back down on the bench. His face was pale. He looked ill. 'I...'

'What is it? Are you okay?' Jess asked.

He looked up at her and she could see dismay in his blue eyes. 'April?'

Jess nodded.

'I wasn't in Australia then,' he said.

'What? I thought you were going back to university?'

Lucas was shaking his head. 'That was my plan. But my plans changed. I went home but I couldn't settle into uni. The father of one of my mates offered me a job in his new hotel and I jumped at the chance. It was a fantastic opportunity, I was going to get to do everything from housekeeping to bartending to running the activities desk and administration, so I took a year off uni. That April, I was in Indonesia.'

'I was looking in the wrong place.' Jess sat on the bench beside him. She was close to tears. All that time spent searching for Lucas, only to find now that she'd been looking in the wrong haystack.

'I'm sorry, JJ. I should have written like I'd planned to, but I thought I had time. I hadn't expected consequences.'

'Neither of us did, I guess,' she sighed. 'But I had to deal with the consequences and I've done the best I could.'

'But what about more recently? Did you look for me again?'

'Of course. I was eighteen, pregnant and alone—do you think I wanted to do this by myself? I searched again when Lily was born but I was still concentrating on Australia and the harder I looked without success the more I believed you didn't want to be found. My father told me you wouldn't want a baby, that you wouldn't want to become a father with a girl you barely knew, and I didn't want to believe him but in the end I didn't have a choice. I couldn't find you.'

'Lily is my daughter.' Lucas stood up and Jess could see him physically and mentally settling himself. He straightened his back and squared his shoulders and focused his forget-me-not-blue eyes on her. 'I need to speak to the doctor.'

'What for?'

'You said he was asking about allergies and family history. We need to tell him to test Lily for celiac disease.'

'What? Why?'

'I'm a celiac and if I really *am* her father then there's a good possibility she has it too.'

'Lucas…' Jess was about to say 'Trust me' but she decided that was a poor choice of phrase. 'Believe me, you're her father.'

'You said Lily had a lot of parties last week. If she has celiac disease and she's overloaded on gluten, that could explain the vomiting. We need to let the doctor know. He needs to run tests.'

'What sort of tests?' Jess felt she should know the answers but it was strange how everything she'd ever learnt seemed to have vanished from her head. Right now she was a patient's mother, not a nurse, and her head was filled with thoughts of Lily and Lucas. There was no room in it for facts about a disease she'd never had to deal with. A disease that quite possibly her daughter had inherited from her father.

Jess needed to focus. Lily was the priority here; she'd have to sort through all the other issues later, when her head had cleared and the dust had settled.

'I think it's just a blood test initially,' Lucas was saying. 'It's been fifteen years since I was diagnosed. We'll have to speak to the doctor.'

He headed back into the hospital with Jess at his heels. Dr Davis was standing beside the triage desk.

'Do you have the CT results?' Jess asked.

He nodded. 'There was no sign of a blockage on the CT scan either.'

'We'd like you to test Lily for celiac disease,' Lucas said.

'Why?' he asked Jess. It was his turn to be puzzled now.

'Apparently her father has celiac disease,' Jess replied.

Dr Davis frowned. 'And you didn't think to tell me?'

'I didn't know.'

'Lily is my daughter,' Lucas interrupted, 'and I have celiac disease.'

'She's never been tested?' Dr Davis asked.

'We were estranged,' Jess said.

At the same time Lucas said, 'I didn't know I had a daughter.'

Neither of the answers made things any clearer for the doctor.

'Look, that's all irrelevant,' Lucas continued. 'The bottom line is I have celiac disease, Lily is my daughter and her symptoms sound consistent with celiac disease. Even if she was asymptomatic, there's a high possibility she has it too. We'd like her tested.'

Dr Davis was nodding now. They'd managed to get his attention but if Jess thought she was going to be the one in control she was mistaken. Lucas was used to being in charge; she'd forgotten how much he relished it and he didn't mince his words with the doctor. He'd become like a wild animal protecting his offspring and nothing was going to stop him from getting what he wanted for Lily. Not this doctor and certainly not her.

If Lucas thought there was a strong chance that Lily had celiac disease they needed to find out for sure, but listening to him now and looking at his body language she knew that if she thought he would bow out of their lives, out of Lily's life, without a whimper, she was mistaken. She knew he would want to be involved, she knew he would fight for Lily, but where would that leave her?

'A blood test isn't conclusive. There are other digestive diseases with similar presentations,' the doctor explained.

'I know that but it's a start,' Lucas replied.

'What do you test for?' Jess asked.

'The best test is the tTG-IgA test. It's the most sensitive and is positive in about ninety-eight per cent of patients with celiac disease.'

'Positive for what?'

'Tissue transglutaminase antibodies. They'll be present if the celiac patient has a diet that contains gluten. But if they've already been avoiding gluten you may get a false negative. Does Lily eat food that contains gluten?'

Jess nodded.

'The result might still depend on whether or not she eats *enough* gluten.'

'It's our best chance,' Lucas insisted. 'Can you run the test?

'I can order it but I'm also going to admit her overnight. I want to keep her here while we run the tests. If it turns out to be appendicitis or a bowel blockage, she's better off here. I'll go and make the arrangements.'

'Now what?' Jess asked Lucas, as they watched the departing figure of the doctor.

'We wait. The important thing is finding out what's wrong with Lily. Celiac disease isn't life-threatening but if left untreated or undiagnosed it can cause irreversible damage to her small intestine. You know that—you're a nurse. If that's all it is it can be controlled by diet. Just cut out gluten. It's much easier to manage now than it was years ago. The important thing is to get it diagnosed.' He ran his hands through his hair, making it more tousled than it normally was. He sighed and shook his head. 'I'm going to wait outside. Come and get me if there's any news.'

That didn't sound like he wanted company.

He headed for the exit and Jess waited inside. Alone. And wondered if she'd done the right thing. But she'd done what she'd had to for Lily's sake.

Lily was brought back from the radiology department and Jess sat with her as the nursing staff got her settled into a ward bed. Her blood was taken and a sedative was added to her drip and Jess stayed with her until she fell asleep.

Lily hadn't vomited since they'd arrived at the hospital and Jess would have been happy to take her home. She would have gladly put all this behind them but the doctor's reasons for admitting Lily were valid ones. She would stay at the hospital for as long as it took to diagnose Lily's problem. But what about Lucas? Had he waited? Was he still in the hospital or had he got out while he still could? She couldn't have blamed him, her announcement must have come as quite a shock. She should have broken the news differently.

She owed him an apology.

She found him sitting on a bench outside the emergency department with his head in his hands. He lifted his head as she sat beside him but he didn't look at her. He ran his hands through his hair as he stretched his legs out, before tipping his head back and resting it against the wall. He was casually dressed in jeans and lace-up workman's boots with a T-shirt under his coat. His hair was tousled but his infectious grin was missing. What had she done?

He sighed and finally looked at her. His forget-me-not-blue eyes were dark purple. He looked exhausted. 'You should have told me.'

'I know.'

'I understand you couldn't find me but for the past two weeks I've been right here. You've had plenty of opportunity to say something and you still chose not to. Why? Why would you continue to keep this a secret? Did you not think I deserved to know I had a child?'

'I was waiting for the right time. I didn't know what you'd think. I needed to find out what kind of person you had become. I didn't know if you wanted to be a father. If you didn't want Lily then she would be better off never knowing about you. Better that than for her to know that her father didn't want her.'

'Of course I would want her. How could you think otherwise?'

'You don't miss what you've never had. She might not matter to you.'

'How can you say that? Of course she matters, and think of all the things I've missed. I missed her being born, I missed her starting school, losing her first tooth, taking her first step, saying her first word. My God, JJ, I don't even know when her birthday is.' He listed all the milestones that Jess had witnessed. She hadn't taken them for granted but she had revelled in them.

'Her birthday is September thirteenth.'

He ignored her olive branch. 'And what about Lily?' he continued, as if she hadn't spoken. 'You thought I wouldn't miss her but what about her? Do you think she doesn't miss having a father?'

Jess had felt the absence on Lily's behalf and Lily herself commented when she saw her friends' families. But did she really know what she was missing? Jess suspected she did—Lily knew what other people's fathers were like. She just didn't know her own.

He had made a good point.

'Yes, she misses it,' she admitted. 'She would love to have a father. She would love you.' Jess could feel tears of regret welling in her eyes but she tried to fight them back. She didn't want to turn on the waterworks, she didn't want Lucas to think she was looking for sympathy—she didn't deserve sympathy. But she did hope to make him understand. She was scared that if he didn't understand he was going to hate her, and how would she live with that?

'And when she asked about her father? What were you planning on telling her?'

'I hadn't worked that out yet. I didn't think we'd ever see you again.' Jess's voice was quiet. There were so many things she'd refused to think about. So many things she'd just tried to ignore. It looked like those days were over now.

'Did you think you were the only one who could love her?'

Jess shook her head. 'No.' *But I was worried you wouldn't love me.*

'I thought I knew you, JJ. I came back here to prove myself to you but I wasn't prepared for this.'

'What are you going to do?'

'I don't know but I want to see Lily.'

'What are you going to say?' Jess was worried. Was she about to lose everything?

'Nothing yet,' he said as he stood up. 'I'm not an idiot. This is a shock for me, it's going to be a shock for her too. I just want to see my daughter. Is that too much to ask?'

Jess shook her head and walked with him to the ward. She hesitated outside the door to Lily's room.

'Aren't you coming in?' Lucas asked.

'I wasn't sure whether you wanted me to.'

'Lily might think it's odd if she wakes up to find me by her bed. You're the one she'll be looking for.'

Lily was still asleep. Lucas stood by her bed. He didn't speak, just stood and watched her. Jess knew that feeling. She used to spend hours just watching Lily sleep when she'd been a baby. She looked like a little angel.

She stirred and murmured. She opened her eyes and recognised Jess but didn't wake fully. 'I need Ozzie,' she said.

Jess pulled the little grey koala with white-tipped ears and a shiny black nose out of her handbag and tucked it under Lily's arm. Lily never liked sleeping without Ozzie. She hugged the soft toy into her chest and closed her eyes again.

'Is that…?' Lucas spoke.

Jess nodded. It was the koala he'd given her for her eighteenth birthday seven years ago.

'You've kept it?'

'It was all I had of you.' Jess could hear the catch in her throat. The little koala had been the cutest thing she'd ever seen, aside from Lucas, and it had become her most treasured possession throughout her pregnancy, and now it was Lily's.

'Does Lily know where you got it?'

'No.' Jess shook her head and turned as she heard the door open.

Dr Davis stepped into the room and he held a piece of paper in his hand. 'I have the blood-test results,' he told them. 'Lily has tested positive for TTG antibodies and the test also showed elevated antigliadin antibodies.

'What does that mean?'

'It means Lily *could* have celiac disease.'

'Could?'

'The blood test isn't definitive,' he reminded her.

'So what do we do now?'

'You can take her home once this drip has run through, provided she has something to eat and keeps it down.'

'She doesn't need to stay overnight?'

'No. With her history and the blood test and scan results I think a bowel obstruction is unlikely so provided she eats, doesn't vomit and can urinate, you can take her home. But she will need an endoscopy and biopsy of her small intestine in order to confirm the diagnosis.'

'A biopsy? What for?'

'To look for inflammation of the intestinal lining and changes to the villi. That's a more definitive indication of celiac disease. Lily will need to see a specialist for the endoscopy. It will be done under a GA. I'll organise a referral. Has she seen a gastroenterologist in the past?'

Jess shook her head. 'No.'

'Who would you recommend?' Lucas asked. 'Who is the best paediatric gastroenterologist in Vancouver?'

'Stuart Johnson.'

Jess had known that would be the answer. 'Is there anyone else?' she asked.

'Of course,' Dr Davis replied, 'but you asked who the best is and in my opinion Dr Johnson is. But I can give you some other names if you prefer.'

Lucas jumped in before Jess could protest any further. 'He will be fine. We'll take that referral.'

'Okay. Do you have any other questions? I'm not an expert but at this stage I wouldn't panic. It looks like celiac disease may be the problem and if that's the case it's one of the easier gastrointestinal problems to control. Just make sure you keep Lily eating some gluten. If you stop before she sees the specialist they may not be able to make an accurate diagnosis. If she has a diet that is already low in gluten we could see a false negative. The recommendation is that she should continue to eat two slices of bread, or the equivalent amount of gluten, per day.'

Lucas waited until the doctor had left the room before he turned to Jess. She knew what he was about to say.

'What is the matter with Stuart Johnson?' he asked. 'Do you know him? Is he a relative? What's wrong with him?'

'He's my father.'

'Your father! Your father is a gastroenterologist?'

'Yes.'

'And he's the top dog?'

'What's going on, JJ? If your father is the best in his field, why did you ask for a different referral? Why don't you want to take Lily to him?'

Jess had managed to delay the discussion until Lily had been discharged and they were in Lucas's car on the way home. Lily seemed to have fully recovered from whatever it was that had upset her. There was no trace of the vomiting, she'd had a good sleep and appeared to have no lingering ill-effects. Jess, on the other hand, was exhausted, physically and emotionally, but she knew Lucas wasn't going to let matters lie.

Lily was cuddling Ozzie while she listened to Lucas's Christmas music through the headphones on his cell phone when he raised the subject again, and Jess figured she might as well get the conversation over with while Lily was out of earshot and otherwise occupied. Maybe it would be easier if Lucas was concentrating on driving and couldn't interrogate her or pin her down with eye contact. 'What do you remember about my father?' she asked.

'That's a loaded question. The only time I came across him was on your birthday when he called me all sorts of colourful names and threw me out. You probably don't want to know my impressions of him as a person.'

'And you're asking why I don't want him to be Lily's specialist?'

'If he's the best in the business then I assume his behaviour that night isn't a reflection on his skills as a doctor. I'm prepared to separate the two. If he's the best I want him to see Lily.'

'My father and I aren't in contact any more.'

'What?' Lucas slowed the car as he took his eyes off the road and looked at her. 'At all?'

Jess shook her head.

'Since when?'

'Since Lily was born. I haven't seen him for six years. He's never met Lily.'

Lucas flicked his gaze back to her a second time. 'If we are going to have any chance of working things out between us, for Lily's sake, we need to operate on a policy of full disclosure. No more secrets. I think it's time you told me everything.' His hands were tight on the steering-wheel and Jess could hear in his voice the effort he was making to stay calm.

She took a deep breath and said, 'Remember I told you how Stephen's death shaped us into the family we became? How I was protected, supervised, guarded almost, from that day on? I went to school, I spent time with Kristie and we came up here as a family. I went to parties but only if Dad had thoroughly researched the event. I understood his reasons—he was determined to do everything he could to keep me safe—and it didn't really bother me until I met you.

'That was when I finally understood Kristie's point of view when it came to boys. For the first time I was prepared to disregard my parents' wishes. For the first time I was prepared to take risks, to ignore their rules, to lie to them or to my aunt and uncle. I couldn't resist you and I couldn't forgive my father for dragging me away from you, for separating us. You were my first love. I couldn't resist you and I gave you everything. My heart and my soul.'

'You gave me everything except for our child,' Lucas said, as he glanced in the rear-vision mirror.

Jess clenched her hands in her lap as she willed herself not to cry. Lucas's words were like a sledgehammer against her already brittle heart and she could feel how close it was to shattering. She had done her best but it didn't seem as though he was prepared to believe that. Maybe, given time, he would trust her again. She'd never deliberately kept Lily from him and maybe one day he would realise that.

She checked back over her shoulder to where Lily lay with her eyes closed. She was either sleeping or listening to music but either way she wasn't paying them any attention. Jess needed Lucas to understand what had happened. She needed to try to explain.

'That's not fair. I told you I tried to find you. If my father had had his way you wouldn't have Lily now either. She is the reason I haven't seen him for six years.'

'Lily is?'

Jess nodded. 'My relationship with Dad had been strained ever since we left Moose River. He was still furious that I'd lied to my aunt and uncle and that I hadn't followed the rules, and finding out I was pregnant was the icing on the cake. I thought that maybe it would be good news, maybe it would help to ease the pain of Stephen's loss, but Dad was convinced it was going to ruin my life. He didn't want me to keep the baby and, as I've explained, he convinced me that you wouldn't want to be a father. He used the argument that you'd never tried to contact me. He was quite persuasive and I even started to question whether you'd given me your real name.'

'Of course I had.'

'I know that now but you have to understand that I was only eighteen and not a very mature eighteen. I was naive and uncertain and scared, and Dad's argument was quite convincing.'

'What did he want you to do? Did he want you to terminate the pregnancy?'

'No! He would never have asked me to do that. We may have had our differences of opinion on lots of things but that wasn't one of them. After losing a child of his own, he wouldn't have wanted me to terminate a pregnancy. He wanted me to give the baby up for adoption.'

'But why?

'He was worried that I was too young. That having a baby at the age of eighteen would ruin my life, my plans for the future. He tried to convince me that there were other options, that I didn't have to be a single mother. Obviously, I refused to give her up. I hadn't planned on getting pregnant but I had a baby growing inside me and it was my job to protect her. Plus she was yours— I couldn't give her up.

'So I decided to keep the baby and prove to my father that I could manage on my own, that I didn't need his help. I was going to prove I could handle the consequences. It was stupid really. I had no idea about anything but I resented my father for taking me away from you and I wasn't going to let him take my baby as well. So I sacrificed the bond I had with my father for the love I felt for Lily. I told my father I was keeping the baby and if he thought I was making a mistake then I would do it on my own and he need have nothing to do with me or his grandchild.'

'Was it a mistake?'

'I certainly hadn't planned on getting pregnant but being with you wasn't a mistake. And Lily isn't a mistake.' Jess glanced back again at her sleeping daughter. Their daughter. Lily was perfect and Jess had never regretted her decision. 'I was a naive teenager with no clue but a massive stubborn streak. It hasn't been easy but I don't regret it.'

'I'm sorry, JJ. It's been tough on you and I'm sorry to have to ask you this, but don't you think it's time you swallowed your pride and moderated your stubborn streak? Don't you think you should try to sort things out with your father? For Lily's sake?'

Jess shook her head. 'No. Too much has happened. I'm not sure I can go back.' Her entire life had changed and all the decisions she'd made, for the right or wrong reasons, had brought her to where she was now. She didn't think her decisions could be reversed that easily. She didn't know if she could do it. 'Couldn't we just ask for a couple of other names? It would be a lot easier.'

'But your father is the best. You're telling me you don't want your daughter, our daughter, to have the best medical attention we can give her? Because I sure as hell do.'

'Let me make some calls,' Jess begged, as Lucas indicated and turned the car onto Moose River Road.

'Let me see what other specialists I can come up with. Please? Just give me twenty-four hours.'

'I'll do you a deal. I'd like to spend some time with Lily so assuming she's feeling okay tomorrow I will pick her up in the morning and she and I can do something together while you sort out a specialist. We both have some decisions to make.'

Jess was worried. Was this going to be the beginning of deals and bargaining? Was Lily's time now up for negotiation? But she couldn't refuse his request. Not if she wanted to win the argument over the specialist.

Lucas parked his SUV in front of the Moose River Apartments. He carried a drowsy Lily inside for Jess but he didn't stay. He didn't stop under the mistletoe and he didn't speak to Jess again. It was as if he didn't even notice she was there.

Whatever Jess had dreamt of having was surely gone. She wasn't going to get the fairy-tale ending. They weren't going to be the perfect family on a Christmas card. She'd be lucky if she was left with anything at all.

But was that just what she deserved?

CHAPTER TEN

'HOW DID YOU GET ON?'

Lucas spoke to Jess as she walked into the stables behind the lodge but there was no 'Good morning'. No 'How are you?' There were obviously more important things on his mind.

Lily had spent the morning with Lucas while Jess was supposed to be organising a specialist appointment. Lily had chosen to groom Banjo and she barely looked up when Jess arrived. It was obvious that Lily had enjoyed the morning far more than Jess had. She seemed quite content with Lucas's company and Jess knew Lily was smitten with him. Why wouldn't she be? He had that same effect on her. Did neither of them need her? Would they be just as happy with each other? Without her?

Everything was changing and Jess was worried.

Jess shook her head in response to Lucas's question as she tried to stem the rising fear in her belly.

'Lily, why don't you finish up with Banjo and then François can bring you to the restaurant for a hot chocolate when you're all done? Your mum and I have some things we need to talk about.'

'Okay,' Lily said. She barely looked up, content just to be with Banjo.

'Have you made a specialist appointment?' Lucas asked as they left the stable to return to the lodge.

Jess had spoken to Cameron but she'd got nowhere with alternative options. She shook her head. 'I couldn't get anything until well into the New Year,' she admitted. 'The doctors Cameron could call in favours from are both on holidays and Lily's condition isn't considered serious so no one else would squeeze her in.'

'I'm sure your father would see her earlier,' Lucas argued. 'I understand your history with your father—you were eighteen and on your own—but I'm here now and if you think I'm not going to be an active part of Lily's life you're mistaken. One way or another I will make sure she gets a diagnosis and the treatment she needs. If she is a celiac then staying on a gluten diet could be doing her more damage. If she is a celiac she'll feel a whole lot better once gluten is eliminated from her diet and we can't do that until she's had the biopsy. We already have a referral to your father,' he continued. 'If you prefer I'll take Lily. You don't need to come. You owe me this much.'

Jess shook her head. She'd already come to the same conclusion. She didn't want Lily to suffer any more than necessary. She knew what she had to do. 'I know she needs the appointment. I'll make the call but I'll take her. Lily is my daughter. She'll need me there.'

'She is also my daughter and that is something else I wanted to speak to you about. When are we going to tell her the truth?'

'Can it wait until the holidays? There's a lot for her

to digest and I think it will be better if she has time to think about it.' Jess honestly felt it would be better to wait a little longer but she also didn't want to deal with the repercussions.

'I'll wait,' Lucas agreed. 'But only until the end of the school term. She finishes on Friday, right?'

Jess nodded.

'I'll take you both to dinner on Friday night, then,' he said, as he held the door for her to step into the lobby. 'We can speak to her together. I'd like to be able to tell my parents about her before Christmas. I was planning on going back to Australia at the end of the ski season and I would like to take Lily too.'

Jess stopped dead in her tracks. He wanted to take Lily!

Black spots danced in front of her eyes and she thought she might either faint or throw up but if she couldn't stand the idea of giving her baby up at birth there was no way she was going to give her up now after six years of being her mother. She might not be able to deny him but she wasn't going to give up without a fight. She stood up as tall as possible and willed her vision to clear. She clenched her fists and tightened her thigh muscles as she tried to stop her knees from shaking. 'No.'

Lucas was frowning. 'What do you mean, "No"?'

'I left Moose River seven years ago, heartbroken and pregnant. Lily was all I had left.' Her voice was quiet but firm. 'I'm sorry I couldn't find you. I'm sorry I didn't try again. I'm sorry that you never posted me those letters and I'm sorry that you've missed six years of her life. I was foolish and I'm sorry but I'm not going to let you take her away from me. I've lost my brother and my mother and my father. Lily is all I have left. I won't let you take her from me.'

'I don't think you were foolish.'

'You don't?' After everything she'd admitted to he wasn't going to crucify her?

'No.' He shook his head. 'I've never said that.' He put his hand on her elbow and guided her to one of the soft leather couches in the lobby. He sat beside her and put his hand on her knee and only then did Jess stop shaking.

'You've made it this far on your own and from what I can see you've done a great job with Lily. She's a great kid and she's lucky enough to have a mother who loves her. I admit I wish I'd known about her before now but I know I have to take some of the blame for that. And I don't intend to take Lily away from you. I'd like to take her to Australia—she's got a whole family over there who would love to meet her—but I'm only talking about going for a holiday. My life is here now. My business is here and my daughter is here. I'm not going to abandon her and I would never take her from you. I assumed you would come with us.'

'Really?' Relief flooded through Jess and she thought she might burst into tears. Her emotions had been running high for days and being close to tears was almost becoming a permanent state for her. 'Even after everything I've done?'

'What's done is done, JJ,' he replied. 'We can't undo the past. We need to move on and Lily has to be our priority. She's the important one. We need to do what's best for her. We need to make sure she feels loved and secure and we need to sort out her health. So will you make an appointment to take Lily to see your father?'

'Yes.' She had no choice. She owed it to Lily and to Lucas. She would have to mend the relationship with her father. After seven years of making all her own decisions it seemed as though her time was up. Fate, or maybe Lucas, was taking over.

Jess was sweating as she picked up the phone and dialled her father's office number. She had never forgotten it, even after all these years. She just hoped he still had the same secretary. How would she explain her request if her father's admin staff had changed?

She'd delayed phoning her father's office until this morning. She'd spent last night trying to work out how to word her request. It seemed strange to be calling to ask for a favour from her father when she hadn't spoken to him in over six years. But it looked like it was time for Jess to be the bigger person and put her stubborn streak to one side, as Lucas had suggested.

She sighed with relief when Gabrielle answered. Jess launched into the speech she'd rehearsed before she could chicken out and she had just hung up the phone when there was a knock on her door. It opened and Cameron stepped in to her clinic room.

'Jess, has Lily gone on the school excursion to go dog sledding?'

What a strange question. Jess frowned and nodded.

'I don't want you to panic, everyone is okay at this stage, but there's been an accident.'

You couldn't tell someone not to panic right before delivering that sort of news. Jess shot out of her seat. 'What is it? What's happened?'

'There's been an accident on one of the chairlifts.'

Jess's hand flew to her mouth as her heart plummeted in her chest. *'Lily.'*

'The children are all okay at this stage but the lift has stopped working and there are people trapped in the cars. I thought you might want to go up the mountain. I'm sure the authorities will contact everyone but I wanted you to know.'

Jess changed her shoes and grabbed her coat. She didn't need to be asked twice.

She raced out of the building and collided with Lucas.

'What are you doing here?' She looked up at him as his arms went around her to steady her. One look at his face told her that he'd heard about the accident too. Of course, he was part of the search and rescue unit.

'What have you heard?' she asked.

'Not a lot at this stage except that no one seems to be injured yet and that a group of six- and seven-year-olds are involved. I thought that might mean Lily. But no one will notify me because I'm not her next of kin. I didn't know if you would call me so I came to you.'

'Have you been called in to the rescue?'

He shook his head and let her go. 'No, this is a mission for the trained team. I came to find out if Lily was in the gondola and to take you up the mountain.' He gestured to his left where a snowmobile was parked at the bottom of the steps. 'It'll be faster than taking the chair lift to the basin and then walking.'

She didn't waste time arguing. She pulled a knitted cap from her pocket and tugged it onto her head as Lucas handed her a pair of snow goggles. She followed him down the steps and climbed onto the snowmobile behind him. She tucked herself against his back and wrapped her arms around his waist. He was solid and muscular. He felt safe. Maybe he really was her knight in shining armour after all.

There was no denying he was a good man. Maybe they would be okay. She and Lucas would work things out. She'd make sure of it. For Lily's sake.

After several minutes Jess felt the snowmobile slow and knew they'd reached the basin. She peered around Lucas's shoulder and saw a group of people, parents of children in Lily's class, gathered around the base of one of the gondola pylons.

Lucas switched off the engine. The lift was motionless and the silence was eerie. Jess had expected noise and activity but everyone seemed to be standing around. Immobile. Uncertain.

They dismounted and Jess removed her goggles. She needed a clearer picture.

They were close to the edge of a gully. The gondola cable stretched across the ravine and Jess's eye was drawn to where it dipped lower. She could see what looked like two cars close together. Weren't they normally further apart than that? Or was she just looking at it from a funny angle?

'What's going on? Why isn't anything happening?' she asked Lucas.

'I'm not sure. I'll go and find out.'

He was back within minutes, bringing Fleur and her husband, Nathan, with him. Fleur's eyes were puffy and her nose was red but she wasn't crying at the moment. Jess hugged her tightly. 'Where are the girls?' she asked.

Fleur pointed down into the ravine to where it looked as though two cars had collided. 'They're in one of those cars.'

'Oh, no!'

'The girls are okay, JJ,' Lucas told her. 'There's a teacher in the gondola with them and she is in contact via her cell phone. No one is badly injured. The second car hasn't come loose but access is difficult.'

Jess released Fleur and turned to Lucas. 'When will they get them out?'

'It's going to take time. It's complicated. No one is getting out of any of the cars until the rescue team are certain that it is safe to do so. They're worried that emptying or moving the cars that haven't been involved in the derailment may cause the unstable cars to fall.'

'They could fall?' Jess clutched Lucas's arm.

'At the moment they think the cars are stable.'

'At the moment! I don't understand how this could happen. How is something like this even possible?'

'Apparently the emergency brake was accidentally activated, which caused one car to derail. The grip holding that car to the cable must have been faulty and when the cable jolted the car bounced and the grip released, but when it slid back into the other car they locked together and so far that has prevented it from falling. But because of where the cars are, getting to them will be tricky. They're talking about rigging up a second cable from tower to tower so that the mountain rescue team can access the gondolas from above. They'll have to secure the cars and then use harnesses and stretchers to lower everyone to safety. It's going to take time,' he repeated.

Jess wrapped her arms around herself. Despite the chill in the air she could feel herself breaking into a sweat. Fear gripped her heart and squeezed it tight. She couldn't bear to think of all the things that could go wrong. She couldn't bear to think of Lily up there, scared and in danger.

Lucas pulled her against his chest. She didn't want to imagine going through this on her own. Whatever happened, she knew she could rely on him. He would be there for Lily and she knew he'd be there for her too. He had promised her that much. She needed to give him something in return.

'If Lily is okay I promise I will give you whatever you want,' she said as she looked up at him. 'We'll tell her the truth tonight.'

Lucas hated feeling useless. He hated not being needed. He'd organised the lodge to send up hot refreshments but that had been the sum total of his assistance, and he wished there was more he could do. Standing around waiting while other people were being constructive didn't sit well with him. His child was trapped in one of the cars and he could do nothing.

He knew this rescue required the expertise of trained personnel and he didn't want to put anyone at risk by having people who were not fully qualified sticking their oar in, and that included him, but it didn't stop him from feeling inadequate.

Fleur and Nathan had gone to get something to eat, leaving him alone with Jess. She hadn't wanted to join the larger group of parents who waited anxiously to hug their children. She said she didn't want to talk to anyone. She sat on the snowmobile and chewed her lip while he paced around in the snow.

The whole process was slow going. Lucas and Jess had been on site for two hours and the gondolas had only just been secured. It was bitterly cold and unpleasant but no one was going anywhere. Hot drinks, soup and blankets were being passed around to the parents and some shelters had been brought up the mountain in an attempt to provide some protection from the biting wind. The wind was blowing straight up the gully, rocking the cars. The wind was strengthening and in Lucas's opinion the rescue team had managed to secure the cars just in time. Any longer and the wind would have made the project even more difficult, treacherous even, but at least the sky was clear. No snow was forecast and that was something to be grateful for. That was one less thing for the mountain rescue team to have to contend with.

'Do you want to sit down for a while?' Jess asked him.

He shook his head. 'I can't sit still. I'm finding it hard enough knowing that other people are being useful while I'm hanging around, twiddling my thumbs.'

Jess had promised him that if they got through this they would tell Lily the truth and he had to believe that everything would be okay. But it was proving difficult. He'd only just discovered the truth and he wasn't prepared to have Lily taken away from him now. 'I wish there was more I could do.'

'You're helping me.' Jess smiled up at him and reached out one hand.

'How?' he asked as he took her hand in his.

'It's nice to know I'm not alone. I'm glad you're here.'

He let her pull him down to sit beside her on the snowmobile. He wrapped his arm around her shoulders and tried to be content with the moment while avoiding thinking about all the things that could go wrong. He could sit still if Jess needed him to. She could anchor him. Sitting with her tucked against his side would settle him.

'Talk to me about Lily,' he said. Talking might keep his mind occupied. It might keep him too busy to worry and there was so much he didn't know about his daughter. He was still coming to terms with the idea that he was a father. He felt the weight of responsibility, to both Lily and Jess, but he was looking forward to the changes this development would bring. He didn't expect it to be easy.

There was a lot he and Jess needed to sort out but he was determined they would manage. He wished he hadn't missed six years of his daughter's life but that was as much his fault as Jess's and all he could do now was make certain he got to share the rest with them both. He refused to think that he wasn't going to get that chance and, in the meantime, he needed to learn as much about Lily as he could. He needed to get to know his daughter.

'She was born at half past six in the morning, six twenty-eight, to be exact, and she weighed seven pounds, five ounces.' Jess's voice lifted as she spoke about their daughter. This conversation wasn't just helping him. It was keeping her mind occupied too. 'She was in a hurry and she didn't come quietly. She hasn't been afraid to let me know what she's thinking ever since. She can be quite stubborn.'

Lucas smiled. 'Sounds like someone else I know.'

Jess nudged him in the side and said, 'She's got plenty of you in her as well.'

'Really?' He was surprised at how pleased he was to hear that. 'Good traits, I hope?'

'Mostly,' Jess teased. 'She's becoming quite a confident skier. I suspect she got her sense of balance from you, and her fearlessness—those things definitely didn't come from me. She has a very strong sense of self and have you noticed she has your ears?'

'I'm glad she got a little bit of me. There's no doubting she's your daughter, but it's nice to know I had something to do with it.'

'Don't worry, there's plenty of you in her. Her eyes aren't always green, they change colour depending on what she wears and if she wears blue they can look like yours. She started walking when she was thirteen months old and lost her first tooth at the beginning of this year. She loves roast chicken and carrots and Disney princesses and her koala and your horse, Banjo. Her favourite colour is pink and she loves to sing.'

Jess paused as around them noise started building. Low murmurs became a buzz of anticipation and people were on the move. The rescue crews in their bright yellow jackets were going past, carrying harnesses, and the ski patrol and ambos carried stretchers and first-aid kits. Lucas knew what that meant.

He stood and reached for her hand. 'They're starting to evacuate the cars.'

They hurried closer and stood waiting. The derailed car was the first to be evacuated but eventually it was Lily's turn.

Jess burst into tears when she spied Lily being lowered from the gondola in a harness. She ran through the snow and scooped her into her arms.

'My precious girl, are you all right?'

'I'm fine, Mum.' She was beaming. 'That was the best excursion *ever*.'

'She sounds okay to me.' Lucas grinned but relief washed over him too.

Jess laughed and wiped the tears from her cheeks. 'You've only been on one other excursion, Lil.' She brushed Lily's hair from her forehead and dropped a kiss there. Her fingers ran gently over the spot she'd just kissed. 'You've got a nasty bump on your head here—are you sure you're okay?'

'I was leaning on the window when the other gondola car crashed into us and I bumped my head. You should have heard the big bang it made.'

'Your head or the car?' Lucas asked.

Lily giggled. 'The car. It sounded like thunder and we all fell on the floor.'

Snow cats had been sent up the mountain to ferry the children back to the medical centre, where they would be checked for any injuries, frostnip or concussion. Jess climbed into the vehicle with Lily, she wasn't prepared to let her out of her sight, and Lucas took the snowmobile back down the mountain and met them at the clinic.

'Is she *still* talking?' he said, as he watched Lily gossiping with a group of friends as they drank hot chocolate and waited to be given the all-clear after their ordeal.

'The whole adventure has given her plenty to say. This is the most excitement she's ever had. She definitely takes after her father.' Jess spoke quietly but her words were accompanied by a smile. 'I always avoided drama.'

'Nature versus nurture?' he asked.

'It looks that way.'

Lucas took Jess's arm and gently pulled her to one side of the bustling waiting room. The noise level was high and he was fairly sure they could talk without being overheard but he made sure he kept Lily within sight. For Jess's sake and his own. 'Will you bring her over to the lodge when you're finished here? I'd like to talk to her tonight.'

Jess frowned and a little crease appeared between her eyebrows, making her look exactly like her daughter. Their daughter. 'I don't know. Don't you think she's had enough for one day?'

'I was as worried as you were up on the mountain, JJ. I want to be part of Lily's life and I want that to start today. I don't want any more missed moments. She's resilient. Look at how she coped with the events of today. She'll cope with this. Besides, it's good news.'

Jess paused and Lucas held his breath. He didn't want to wait. He wanted to be acknowledged as Lily's father.

Finally she nodded. 'All right. I'll take her home for a warm bath and then we'll come over.'

'Lily, your mum and I have something to tell you.'

Lily paused momentarily with one hand on Banjo's neck. It had been Jess's suggestion that they go to the stable and he had agreed without reservation. Grooming Banjo was a soothing, familiar activity for Lily and it meant they didn't have to sit awkwardly in the hotel to have this conversation. 'Is it a surprise?' she asked. 'I love surprises.'

'It was a surprise for me,' Lucas told her. 'But it's something I'm very excited about. Something I've wished for for a long time.'

'Lil, you know how I've always said you were made up of bits and pieces?' Jess asked her,

Lily nodded and tilted her head as she replied, 'Like a platypus.'

'That's right. Well, the outside bits of you are just like me,' Jess said, 'but some of the inside bits of you are different. Parts of your insides are funny and other parts are curious and other parts are brave, much braver than me, and you get those parts from your dad.'

Lily frowned and Lucas was reminded of how Jess had looked earlier in the day. 'I don't have a dad.'

'Everyone has a dad somewhere, sweetheart. I just lost your dad for a while and it took me a long time to find him again.'

'Is he nice?'

'He's very nice.'

Jess smiled at Lucas as she spoke to their daughter, and Lucas finally had what he'd wished for. He remembered the expression on Jess's face the night she'd told him about her relationship with Lily's father. How she'd looked when she'd told him that she'd loved Lily's dad. He'd seen the love in her eyes that night and he'd wished she'd been talking about him. He hadn't known then that he was Lily's father but she had that same expression in her eyes tonight. She'd said she loved him then. Did she love him still?

'Will he like me?' Lily wanted to know.

'He will *love* you. Very much. But I think he might want to tell you that himself.'

'When can I see him?'

'He's right here, Lily.'

'Where?'

'It's me, Lily,' Lucas told her 'I'm your dad.'

'Really?'

'Really.' He nodded. 'And I think I'm the luckiest dad in the world.'

'This is the best day ever,' Lily said, as she threw her arms around his neck and burrowed in against his chest.

He'd been worried about her reaction to their news. Holding his child in his arms was the most incredible feeling and he would have been devastated if Lily hadn't wanted him. He didn't think he would be able to give her up after this. What would he have done if she hadn't been as thrilled about the news as Jess had assured him she would be? What if she hadn't been as excited as he'd hoped she would be?

He wondered how Jess was feeling. He looked over the top of Lily's head. Jess was smiling but he could see a glimmer of tears in her eyes. How did she feel about having to share Lily?

Lily had fallen asleep on his couch after polishing off her dinner. Lucas looked at his sleeping daughter. Her blonde head was resting on Jess's lap and she had Ozzie, the koala, tucked under her arm. She was beautiful. She was perfect.

'What is it?' Jess asked him.

'I think it's incredible that we made her.' He'd never felt that anything was missing in his life but now that Jess was back in it, and Lily too, he wondered how he could not have known that there should be more. 'And that she accepted me so easily.'

'She thinks you're fabulous.'

'She does?'

'Why wouldn't she? You own a horse and sleigh.' Jess was smiling at him and his heart swelled with love for her and their daughter. His family.

He needed to make that his reality.

Thinking of family made him think of hers. 'Have you spoken to your father yet?'

Jess shook her head. 'Not exactly. But I did speak to his secretary this morning. Luckily she's been working for him for ever and she has booked Lily in for the biopsy on the Wednesday before Christmas. I meant to tell you but with all the drama today I forgot,' she said as she stifled a yawn.

'But you didn't speak to your father.'

'No. I couldn't do it. Talking to him on the phone didn't seem right but I don't know what to do. I don't want to have our first conversation in six years just before Lily goes into the operating theatre—that won't be any good for any of us—but I'm running out of time.'

'Sleep on it,' he said, as she stifled another yawn. 'A solution will present itself.' He had an idea that might just work. 'And why don't you take my bed for the night?' he offered. 'There's no point in waking Lily to take her home.'

Jess shook her head. 'Thanks, but if you bring me a blanket I'll be perfectly happy to sleep in front of the fire. I need to stay close to her, I don't want her to wake up in unfamiliar surroundings without me. Not after the day she's had.'

'I'll move her to my bed, then, and I'll take the couch.'

He picked Lily up. She was feather-light in his arms and snuggled in against his chest, still fast asleep. Jess followed him into his bedroom and pulled the comforter back. He tucked Lily under it before dropping a kiss on her forehead.

They stood together and watched Lily sleep. 'I still can't quite believe I have a daughter. It's incredible.

Thank you, JJ. For giving me this gift. For being strong enough to make what must have been a tough decision. Do you mind sharing Lily with me?'

Jess shook her head. 'Of course not. I never wanted to do this on my own and having you in Lily's life will be a good thing for her—provided we can figure out how it's all going to work.'

'We will,' he agreed, 'but not tonight. There have been enough decisions made today.' He turned Jess to face him. 'But I do have one more question for you. I want to be a part of your life too.'

'You will be. We'll always be connected through our daughter.'

'I want more than that. I want a chance to have a re- lationship with you that goes beyond us as parents. I want more. I want you.'

'You want me? After everything I've done?'

'Look around you, JJ. Everything I've done has been with you in mind. I know I said I wanted to prove a point to your father but I wouldn't have bothered with that if it wasn't for you. You were the reason I've done this. You were the reason I came back. I admit I've got more than I bargained for but I'm thrilled about that. The past is the past. I meant it when I said there's no point dwelling on it. It can't be changed. We all had a hand to play in the mess we made—me, you and your father—but what's done is done. It doesn't change how I feel about you or Lily. All we can do is look to the future. We have the rest of our lives to make up for lost time.'

'Really?'

'That was my plan.' He was smiling, grinning like a lovestruck fool. He loved her and he wanted to be 'the one' for her. He wanted them to be a family. 'Do you have other plans that I should know about?'

Jess shook her head. 'No.'

'Good.' He took Jess's face in his hands, cupping her cheeks gently between his palms, and tipped her head up. Her green eyes were wide, her lips plump and pink. He wanted her to be his. He wanted to claim her for his own.

He bent his head and covered her lips with his, pouring his love into her and sealing it with a kiss. She tasted like vanilla ice cream, innocent and sweet, and he made a promise to himself that he would take care of her, of her and Lily, if she would let him. He would convince her, he would persuade her, he would charm her and love her until she agreed to give herself to him. And then he would be content.

CHAPTER ELEVEN

JESS'S HEART POUNDED in her chest and her arm felt as if it weighed a tonne as she reached for the door handle of the lodge suite. Her hand was shaking and her palms were clammy. 'I don't think I can do this,' she said to Lucas.

He'd told her he would take care of things but she hadn't expected him to do it so quickly and she also hadn't expected her father to agree to Lucas's suggestion, but it seemed as though she had been wrong on both counts because her father was here, in Moose River, and he was waiting for her.

'It'll be okay, JJ, and I'll be just outside if you need me. Remember, this time I've got your back.' Lucas's voice gave her the courage to turn the handle. 'You can do this.'

She pushed the door open. 'Daddy?'

He was halfway across the room, coming to meet her. He was tall and still trim, although his dark hair was greyer than she remembered. He was sixty now. She'd missed his sixtieth birthday and he'd missed her twenty-first. For what? Why?

Because she was stubborn.

But his arms were open, forgiving, inviting. She

burst into tears and stepped into his embrace. 'I'm sorry, Dad,' she said, as his arms tightened around her. He'd only ever wanted to protect her and she'd repaid him by cutting him out of her life.

She closed her eyes and sobbed and let him hug her as he'd done when she'd been a child. She could feel the tension in her shoulders ease. She could feel the forgiveness in his embrace and all the anxiety that had been building up, all her nervousness over this meeting slipped away as he held her.

'I'm sorry too, Jessie.' He stepped back to look at her, pulling a clean handkerchief out of his pocket and handing it to her.

She smiled through her tears. 'You still carry a handkerchief.' It was one of the many things she remembered about him. Her father wore cufflinks and always had a clean hankie in his pocket.

'Always,' he replied. 'Some things never change. It's good to see you, sweetheart.'

'You too, Dad.' Jess looked around the room. She could smell coffee. There was a pot and two mugs on the sideboard. Only two cups. 'Is Mum here?' she asked.

'No. I wasn't sure how receptive you were going to be. She wouldn't be able to handle any confrontation.'

Jess was disappointed and she felt her shoulders drop. 'I wasn't planning on being confrontational,' she told him. She hadn't been planning anything. This had all been Lucas's idea. But it was silly to feel disappointed about her mother's absence when she hadn't even been sure if she herself wanted to come to the meeting. Why should her mother feel any differently?

Her father must have heard the disappointment in her voice. 'I'm sorry, Jessie. But we'll work it out. This is the first step. I promise I'll do everything I can to make sure we will be a family again.' He reached into his pocket and pulled out his wallet. 'I have something I want to show you.' He flipped his wallet open and handed it to her.

He'd always had a photo of her and Stephen as children in the plastic sleeve but that was gone now. Jess stared at the replacement. Her own eyes stared back at her. The photo was one of her and Lily. It was a photo Kristie had taken on Lily's sixth birthday.

She sat on the sofa and slipped the photo out of the sleeve. Behind it was the old photo of her and Stephen. She held the picture of Lily in her hands and looked up at her father. 'Where did you get this?'

'Kristie gave it to Aunt Carol. She gave it to me.'

'Why?'

'I asked for it.' Her father dragged an armchair across the floor, positioning it at an angle to the sofa, so that he was nearby without crowding Jess. 'I know I wasn't very supportive when you told me you were pregnant and were planning on keeping the baby. I didn't understand how you could make that decision at the age of eighteen but when you cut me out of your life I felt like I'd lost both of my children, first Stephen and then you. Kristie was my link to you, to you and to Lily. I tried to keep in touch with you but when you returned all my letters I had to rely on your aunt and uncle to give me news over the years. I couldn't stand the thought of you being lost to me for ever.'

Her father had sent her a letter, along with a birthday card and a sizeable cheque for Lily, every year. Kristie had always delivered it for them but Jess hadn't realised things had been going back in the other direction. Jess had kept the cards—she had boxed them up and put them away for Lily—but she had returned the letters and the cheques, still determined to prove she could manage on her own. Determined to prove she didn't need anything from her father.

But all this time he'd been hearing about Lily. She didn't know why she was surprised. If she'd ever given it any thought she would have figured out that Aunt Carol would have passed on any information her parents asked for. All this time he'd been following Lily's progress. Despite Jess's actions he had never stopped being her father or Lily's grandfather. He had never given up hope.

'I'm sorry I was stubborn. I'm sorry I've kept you out of our lives,' she apologised. 'I returned your letters but I've kept your cards for Lily. I was going to give them to her one day.' She wanted him to know that. It was important.

'Thank you, Jessie.' Her father reached for her hand and Jess gave it to him. 'I've missed you. Do you think we might have a chance to start fresh?'

'I wasn't sure if I could forgive you for separating me from Lucas. I loved him then, I love him still.' Jess felt her father tense and she hurried to continue, to put his mind at ease. 'But he says we need to leave the past behind if we want to move forward and I think he's right. I would like a chance to start again.' She stood up. 'Would you like to meet Lily?'

'Now?'

Jess nodded.

'She's here?'

'She's in the lodge. Lucas is waiting outside. He'll fetch her.'

'I'd love to, Jessie, and if it's all right I'd like to meet Lucas too. After all, I have him to thank for bringing you back into my life.'

Jess nodded. 'Okay. Give me a minute.' She was smiling as she left the suite. Lucas was waiting for her, just as he'd promised.

'You look happy.'

She walked over to him and threw her arms around him, hugging him tightly.

He picked her up and held her close. 'What was that for?' he asked, as he set her back down on her feet.

'It's a thank-you. I think it's going to be okay. Dad wants to meet Lily.'

'That's good. I've already asked Sofia to bring her up and I've ordered some champagne and afternoon tea for you too.'

'You knew it would go well?'

'I could tell when I spoke to him on the phone that he was keen to reconcile. I was pretty sure this would all turn out okay and I'm glad it has so far.'

'He wants to meet you too.'

'Now?'

Jess nodded and Lucas followed her back into the room.

'Dad, this is Lucas White. Lucas, my father, Stuart Johnson.'

Jess's heart was in her throat. *Please, be nice, Dad.*

Stuart was looking at Lucas closely but he stayed silent. He extended his hand and Jess exhaled as they shook hands. They seemed far more relaxed than she was. Perhaps this would turn out all right after all.

'Good to meet you properly at last, sir. I apologise for not taking responsibility before now—'

Stuart cut him off and Jess held her breath again. 'That's all right. I think I owe you an apology. I was hasty in my judgement of you and it cost me my daughter and my granddaughter. Thank you for bringing them back to me.'

'I want you to know that I intend to make it up to Lily,' Lucas said. 'And to Jess. I have the means and the desire to make it up to both of them and I'm not one to shy away from my responsibilities.'

Lucas stood next to her and she took his hand and squeezed it. He circled her waist with his arm and pulled her close, and Jess could almost feel her life turning around. With Lucas beside her, perhaps things would be okay. With him beside her, anything seemed possible. She'd felt lost, adrift and alone with no one except Lily and Kristie. She never would have admitted it, she was too stubborn, but now perhaps she could. With Lucas back in her life and her father and maybe even her mother, she and Lily wouldn't be alone any more.

Maybe she had a chance of finding happiness after all.

Jess was wearing scrubs and was sitting in the operating theatre at the foot of the bed while her father prepared for Lily's biopsy. The anaesthetist gave Lily a very light general anaesthetic and when she gave Stuart the all-clear he slid a flexible tube, complete with a tiny camera, down Lily's oesophagus, through her stomach and into the small intestine. Jess could watch the images on the monitor above their heads. Stuart examined the intestinal lining and took half a dozen samples at various points.

'What are you looking for?' Jess asked. She'd researched the procedure and the disease and she knew she was asking just to hear her father's voice. It was hard to believe he was back in her life.

'Atrophy of the villi and inflammation of the mucosal tissue,' he explained. 'There's a pathologist waiting for the samples as we speak so the results should be back almost immediately.'

The whole process took less than fifteen minutes and the light anaesthetic Lily had been given was reversed quickly. Then it was just a matter of more waiting.

Lucas and Jess were sitting with a drowsy Lily in the day surgery recovery area when Stuart ducked in between surgeries.

He kept his mask on as he spoke to them.

'The results are back. The villi are shrunk and flattened, indicating partial atrophy, and there is an increased presence of lymphocytes and some other changes consistent with inflammation. The Marsh classification is given as Marsh III.'

'What does that mean?'

'It means Lily has celiac disease.'

'Should I have done something about this earlier?' Guilt swamped Jess again.

Her father shook his head. 'From what I've read in her history from the emergency department, any symptoms she did have were so mild they could have been attributed to any number of things. Because it is commonly an inherited condition, finding out Lucas's history was the red flag. I know it's called a disease but you should think of it more as a condition. It's easily controlled as long as you are prepared to be vigilant with Lily's diet. I'm sure Lucas will agree with me, it's not difficult to manage. Once Lily has a gluten-free diet the villi and her intestine will recover.'

'How long does that take?'

'Usually around three to six months, but provided she sticks to a gluten-free diet there won't be any long-term effects. If she doesn't adhere to a strict gluten-free diet there can be other complications but there'll be time to discuss those later. I'll tee up an appointment with a dietician and a counsellor. It'll be okay, Jessie, we'll get through this.' He squeezed her hand. 'I have to get back into Theatre. Will you be all right?'

Jess reached for Lucas's hand and smiled at her father. 'We'll be fine.'

Lily was up bright and early on Christmas morning. She'd had no ill effects following the biopsy and had taken the news about her celiac disease in her stride, just like everything else. In all honesty, Jess suspected Lily was pleased to know that she and Lucas had something tangible in common.

That had been one problem solved. Jess had been busy ticking boxes over the past few days and things were going well. With Lucas's help she was mending her relationship with her parents, both her mother and her father. Lucas had invited them to the lodge for Christmas lunch and they were coming, along with Kristie and her parents. It would be the first family Christmas in many years and Jess and Lily were both excited. Lucas was helping to repair all the damage Jess had done but fortunately everyone seemed prepared to forgive her.

The only other thing still to be finessed was her relationship with Lucas and how they would parent Lily. But Jess knew they would get there. One thing at a time.

Lily was bouncing up and down on Lucas's bed, where she and Jess had spent another night while Lucas had slept on the couch. Jess felt bad about kicking him out of his own bed yet again but he had insisted. He wanted to be there when Lily woke up, he said. He'd missed all of her Christmases to date and he didn't want to miss another one. It was a good argument and Jess had happily agreed.

'Is it time for presents yet?' Lily was asking.

'We'll go and see if your dad is awake.' It was going to take some time to get used to saying that but Jess liked how it sounded.

'Merry Christmas to my girls,' he said, as he kissed them both and handed Jess a coffee.

'Did Santa come?' Lily asked.

'There seems to be a very big present by the fireplace that wasn't there last night,' Lucas was grinning. 'Shall we take a look?'

An enormous gift sat in front of the fireplace and Lily wasted no time in tearing the paper off it to reveal a magnificent doll's house. It was one she had admired at the Christmas market and had working lights and delicate furniture. A curved staircase led from the first to the second floor and a hollow chimney ended in a small fireplace in the lounge that was complete with tiny logs that lit up with fake flames at the flick of a switch. It was elaborate and beautiful.

'I think Santa might have stolen your thunder,' Jess said with a smile as Lily flicked the lights on and off before picking up a tiny music box that was inside the doll's house. She turned the handle on its side and squealed with delight as it played 'Waltzing Matilda'. 'You might not be her favourite today,' Jess added.

'Santa had six years to make up for but I've still got a few tricks up my sleeve.'

He handed Lily a small box. Nestled in tissue paper was a carved wooden sleigh. It had been painted red, just like the Crystal Lodge sleigh. Lily lifted it carefully from the box. Attached to it was a perfect replica of Banjo. 'I love it, Daddy, it looks just like Banjo.'

'Okay, Dad's turn, Lil,' Jess told her, once they'd all finished admiring the tiny horse.

Lily handed Lucas a flat, heavy parcel and then went to play with her doll's house as he unwrapped his gift, revealing a photo album.

He turned the pages of the album. It was filled with photographs of Lily, beginning on the day she'd been born and continuing to her sixth birthday. As Jess described each picture, telling Lucas something about each occasion, Lily's curiosity got the better of her. Fascinated as always by photographs of herself when she'd been younger, she abandoned the doll's house temporarily and climbed onto Lucas's lap. She snuggled against his chest and added to the commentary as he turned the pages. 'That's me when I lost my first tooth,' she said, 'and that's me when I was in the nativity play last year. I was a shepherd. And that's me on the day I started school in Moose River.'

'It's brilliant, JJ,' Lucas said, as he reached the end of the album and closed the book. He leant behind Lily and kissed Jess lightly on the lips. 'Thank you.'

'I have something else for you too,' she said, as she handed him a large, thin envelope. Inside was one sheet of paper.

Lucas slid it out. 'It's Lily's birth certificate.'

Jess nodded. 'I've had it amended,' she said. She

pointed to the word 'Father'. In the box underneath it said 'Lucas White'.

'This is the most perfect gift.'

'It's going to be a perfect Christmas,' Jess replied.

'I hope so. But there's one more thing to do before we reach perfection.'

'What's that?'

'Your present.' Lucas turned to Lily, who had returned to play, and Jess had to smile when she saw that Lily was busy showing mini-Banjo through the house. 'Lil, it's time for Mum's surprise.'

Lily put Banjo down and dived under the Christmas tree to retrieve a gift bag.

Lucas picked up Jess's hand and looked into her eyes. 'JJ, I loved you seven years ago and I love you still. You are beautiful and smart and I never forgot you. I love you and I love Lily. I want us to be a family.' Without letting go of her hand, he got down on one knee beside the couch. Lily was bouncing up and down on the cushion beside Jess, clutching the gift bag. 'Jess Johnson, will you do me the honour of becoming my wife? Will you marry me?'

Jess's eyes filled with tears.

'No! Don't cry, Mum.'

'It's all right, Lil, these are happy tears,' Jess said as she choked back a sob. 'You are my first and only love,' she said to Lucas. 'I have loved you and only you since the moment you first kissed me and, yes, I will marry you.'

Lily threw her arms around them both. 'Hooray,' she shouted.

'Okay, Lily, you can hand over the bag now,' Lucas said, when Lily finally released them.

Inside the bag was a tiny jewellery box. Jess pulled it out and lifted the lid. A princess-cut diamond ring glistened in dark blue velvet. Lucas pulled it from the cushion.

'Just as you have rescued me I promise to always protect you for as long as you need me. I promise to love you and Lily and to keep you safe. Always,' he said, as he slid the ring onto her finger before kissing her.

'I think she likes it,' Lily said, as Jess held her hand out so they could all admire it.

'You knew about this?' Jess asked her.

'Lily helped me choose the ring,' Lucas replied. 'She's nearly as good at keeping secrets as you are.'

'No more secrets. I promise.'

Lily was tugging Jess's arm. 'Now do you think I can have a baby sister?'

Jess smiled and looked into Lucas's forget-me-not-blue eyes. 'We'll see what we can do.'

EPILOGUE

JESS LAY ON a beach towel and let the autumn sun warm her pale skin as she watched Lucas and Lily playing in the famous Bondi surf. Lucas had swapped his snowboard for a surfboard and he was giving Lily her first surfing lesson. She was proving to be a natural, showing Jess once again that nature was just as strong as nurture.

Lucas came out of the water, leaving Lily to practise her surf moves with his youngest brother. He jogged up the beach to Jess and she didn't bother to pretend she wasn't checking him out. They'd been in Australia for a month and Lucas was tanned and fit and gorgeous. And all hers. He stood over her, blocking the sun and giving her a very nice view of his sculpted chest and strong thighs. His board shorts dripped water on the sand as he towelled his hair dry, leaving it even more tousled than normal.

She smiled up at him. 'Lily's having a great time. She's picked it up really fast. She must take after her dad.'

'Your husband,' he said, as he flopped down onto the sand beside her and kissed her.

They had married in Moose River in February and had just celebrated their three-month anniversary with a second ceremony with Lucas's family. It had been a whirlwind few months and Jess was exhausted but elated. She wouldn't change a thing.

'Happy?' he asked.

'Extremely,' she replied, as she rolled onto her side to look at Lucas. Some days she still couldn't believe her good fortune. Lucas was back in her life, he'd given her back her family and he'd given her himself too. She was happy and she had everything she needed. She reached out and picked up her husband's hand. 'But, in the interest of full disclosure, because I promised no more secrets, there is something I need to tell you.'

'Is it that you love me?'

'I do. But that's not a secret.'

'I know, I just like to hear you say "I do".' Lucas laughed and kissed her fingers. 'Sorry, go on.'

'You know how Lily always asks for a baby sister for Christmas? I've been thinking…'

'You think we should make a baby?' Lucas's forget-me-not-blue eyes lit up.

Jess shook her head. 'That wasn't what I was going to say.' She smiled as Lucas's face fell. She knew he was going to love her news. 'It's too late for that. We've already done it.'

'What?'

'I'm pregnant.'

'You are?'

Jess nodded. 'The baby is due the week before Christmas. So it looks as though Lily will get her Christmas wish this year. She's going to have a sibling,' she said, as she brought Lucas's hand to her belly.

'That is fantastic news, JJ. The best.'

'All those things you missed out on with Lily, I

promise you'll be there for every one of them this time around. Do you think that sounds okay?'

'I do.'

Jess closed her eyes and smiled as his lips covered hers.

This was the perfect start to the first day of the rest of their lives.

* * * * *

MILLS & BOON®
Christmas Collection!

**Unwind with a festive romance this Christmas
with our breathtakingly passionate heroes.
Order all books today and receive a free gift!**

Order yours at
**www.millsandboon.co.uk
/christmas2015**

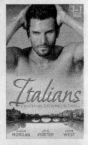

MILLS & BOON®

Why shop at millsandboon.co.uk?

Each year, thousands of romance readers find their perfect read at millsandboon.co.uk. That's because we're passionate about bringing you the very best romantic fiction. Here are some of the advantages of shopping at www.millsandboon.co.uk:

* **Get new books first**—you'll be able to buy your favourite books one month before they hit the shops

* **Get exclusive discounts**—you'll also be able to buy our specially created monthly collections, with up to 50% off the RRP

* **Find your favourite authors**—latest news, interviews and new releases for all your favourite authors and series on our website, plus ideas for what to try next

* **Join in**—once you've bought your favourite books, don't forget to register with us to rate, review and join in the discussions

Visit **www.millsandboon.co.uk** for all this and more today!

MILLS & BOON®

MEDICAL ROMANCE™

THE ULTIMATE IN ROMANTIC MEDICAL DRAMA

A sneak peek at next month's titles...

In stores from 6th November 2015:

- **A Touch of Christmas Magic** – Scarlet Wilson *and*
  Her Christmas Baby Bump – Robin Gianna

- **Winter Wedding in Vegas** – Janice Lynn *and*
  One Night Before Christmas – Susan Carlisle

- **A December to Remember** – Sue MacKay
- **A Father This Christmas?** – Louisa Heaton
